the Rescue *of* Stormie Brown

Deborah Elum

For information, contact:
All That Productions, Inc.
P.O. Box 1594
Humble, Texas 77347-1594

ISBN 978-1-7339510-5-0
Library of Congress Control Number: 2023909849

Dedication

To my brother, Ronnie Thomas who encouraged me to finish this project.

Acknowledgments

I give thanks to God, my Lord Jesus Christ, and the Holy Spirit.

To my husband, Randy, and my son, Brian. They are a blessing and inspiration to me.

To my mother, Lucy Peterson and friend, Emily Smith.

Water Me

Just like a flower needs the rain
And the dew needs the grass
Water me.

Just like a shore needs an ocean
And the tides need the moon
Water me.

As a shadow needs the sun
And sand needs the beach
Water me.

As a seed needs the earth
And a bloom needs a flower
Water me.

- Deborah Elum

CHAPTER ONE

Stormie

I sat in bed, my mind still foggy from sleep, trying to process the fact that my fiancé, Daniel Booker, didn't call me this morning. I felt a sense of dread settle in my stomach, knowing that this was going to be a tough day. As I wiped away the tears, I couldn't help but wonder what had set him off this time.

Daniel and I had made it a routine to talk at five every morning since we started dating. It was our way of staying connected before we left for work, a moment to share our thoughts and feelings. But lately, something had changed.

There were days when our morning conversations didn't happen, when silence permeated the space that used to be filled with the familiar sound of his voice. It wasn't a result of him being preoccupied with work or running late, rather, it was because he was consumed by anger. Whether it was directed at something specific or someone in particular, I could never anticipate.

I couldn't help but take it personally. Deep down, I knew my reaction stemmed from the trauma I endured during my upbringing with my stepfather. The echoes of my past intertwined with the present, clouded my ability to separate myself from the storm of someone else's anger. The wounds from those experiences left me sensitive to any signs of anger or hostility, even if they were unrelated to me.

The memories of the harsh words and unpredictable outbursts inflicted upon me by my stepfather lingered in the back of my mind, shaping my perception of conflict and communication with each new romantic relationship. The echoes of those painful moments had etched themselves into the very fabric of my being, causing me to question and doubt myself whenever anger emerged in Daniel.

It was a constant battle between my rational understanding and the lingering emotional scars. I wanted to believe that Daniel's anger wasn't a reflection of me or my worth, but the insecurities from my past made it difficult to separate the two. Afterward, I longed to hear those three simple words—"I love you"—whenever I faced the brunt of his anger.

As the days crept closer to our wedding, I couldn't help but notice a disturbing trend in Daniel's behavior. Every little thing that didn't go his way seemed to trigger his anger, and it was becoming more frequent. I had noticed it before, of course—his short fuse and tendency to lash out had always been a concern—but lately it seemed to be getting worse.

It was as if he was trying to control everything, down to the smallest detail, and when something didn't go according to plan, he flew into a rage. I tried to talk to him about it, but he always brushed me off, insisting that he was just under a lot of stress and that everything would be fine once the wedding was over.

I knew that I shouldn't have let things get this far. I should have stood up for myself even when we were dating. But I had been so in love with him, so blinded by his charm, that I too had convinced myself things would get better after we got married. He was just experiencing pre-wedding jitters.

Now, I was trapped in a cycle of emotional abuse, with no way out. My eyes swelled up with tears. Soon, tear after tear began to roll down my cheeks and land on my white satin pillow case. I thought *was he angry this time with me or was it someone else?* It was hard to figure him out. He's been so distant and cold lately. I just didn't know what to do.

Daniel possessed everything most women wanted in a man. He was handsome, successful, and intelligent. Yet, despite all he had going for himself, his insecurities caused him to be very harsh towards anyone that made him feel threatened. Unfortunately, I was one of the targets that he used to take out his frustrations. Of course, when we first started dating five years ago, there were warning signs along the way. Like so many women looking for that "good man," I ignored them all. I mean every single one of them. I just chose to believe that I could change him. My commitment and love for him gave me the strength to fight for our relationship.

Memories began to flood my mind as wave after wave of desperation washed over me. I refused to travel the rough seas of what he might do if I ventured too far off course. He said he loved me but he sometimes treated me like he hated me. I felt some days like a wrecked catamaran - damaged, unused, and abandoned. I dared not stand up to him or else risk voyaging into unknown waters. I do not think he had a clue, that for me, it was a daily struggle to keep my sanity.

The alarm clock began to chime briskly returning me back to reality. No sooner as I shifted the button to the off position, the telephone on the night stand began ringing. The sound of the phone ringing startled me out of my thoughts. As I sat up and lifted it to my left ear, a familiar voice on the other end could be heard.

"Hey, girl, how's it going down there in Houston?" Dee Dee hoisted herself from the overstuffed loveseat as I held the telephone firmly wedged between my head and shoulder.

I cleared my throat. Almost in a whisper, "Everything is fine," came quickly. Like my mother, I learned how to cover up my true emotions.

"Hold on, Stormie, for a few seconds while I conference in Liz."

Inside, I was drowning in a sea of emotions, struggling to keep my head above water.

After hearing a few clicking sounds, Liz began saying, "Yes, I'm here. Hey, Stormie. How is the weather in Houston? It's raining cats and dogs here."

Liz giggled, eager to share her story about the amount money she wasted getting her hair done on Saturday. "Money wasted when it rains. Just wasted."

I took a deep breath and tried to sound cheerful. "It's sunny and beautiful here."

Dee Dee's voice grew serious. "Stormie, are you okay? You sound upset."

Liz sighed, frustrated. "I should have waited to get my hair done. Now, I have to get my hair done again. I hope my stylist can work me in. She is usually booked up for two weeks."

"Liz, please would you hold your rambling on for a minute. What's going on, Stormie?"

The habit of covering up my true emotions was too strong. I drew a deep breath and sighed, weary. "I'm fine, girl. You know how stuffy I sound during the springtime with all this pollen in the air."

Dee Dee detected an insincere happiness in my voice. "Listen, chick, stop lying. I can tell it in your voice. Don't pretend with me. I know you too well."

Thunder rumbled outside as goose pimples rose on Liz's arm. "Stormie, are you okay?"

"No, she's not okay," interjected Dee Dee. "I can read that girl like a book."

Dee Dee exhaled, rolled her eyes, and shook her head. "What's going on with you? I bet you it's Daniel, isn't it?"

I hesitated for a moment, wondering whether to open up to my friends or not. But then, I knew I needed their support more than ever. I paused as tears gently rolled down my cheeks again. I could barely get the words out of my mouth. "Yeah, it's him."

One thing for sure was that I could confide in my two best friends. We were more than friends, we were sisters. My friendship with Liz Braxton and Dee Dee Taylor existed since elementary school in College Station, Texas.

After we graduated from Texas A&M University in College Station, each followed different career paths. Dee Dee moved to Mesquite, Texas just fourteen miles east of Dallas and bought a home close to her business. She owned a clothing boutique named, "Dee Dee's Fashion Haven." Dee Dee's dedication to her boutique and her passion for fashion made her boutique a go-to destination for anyone seeking the latest trends and unique pieces. Her boutique had become a staple in the Mesquite retail scene, attracting customers from near and far with its fashionable selections and friendly atmosphere. With her keen eye for style and a curated collection of trendy and unique clothing, her boutique had become a popular destination for fashion enthusiasts even in the Dallas area.

On the other hand, Liz became a flight attendant while also owning an online jewelry business. It allowed her to explore her creative side while embracing the opportunities of her chosen profession. She had the opportunity to explore the world and interact with people from diverse backgrounds. Her warm and friendly personality made her a favorite among passengers, creating a welcoming and enjoyable experience during flights. For convenience, she bought a home in Irving, Texas so she could cut down her commute time to get to and from the airport.

She had the privilege of traveling to various destinations around the world. She relished in the excitement of exploring new cultures, experiencing different fashion trends, and discovering unique pieces of jewelry along the way. Inspired by her global adventures, Liz recognized the potential to share her passion for jewelry with others. With careful research, dedication, and an eye for quality and style, she curated a stunning collection of jewelry pieces from artisans and designers across the globe. Her online platform, named "Glamour

Girl Gems," showcased a wide range of meticulously crafted necklaces, earrings, bracelets, and rings, each one telling its own story and reflecting the diverse beauty of different cultures.

"How is old grumpy anyway?" Dee Dee's asked in a sarcastic tone. "As if I really cared."

"Fine, I guess. I really don't know since he didn't call me this morning." I paused suddenly.

Dee Dee frowned and shook her head again. "I bet you don't even know why, do you?"

I continued, "Not really."

Dee Dee became more enraged by what she heard. She burst into the conversation with fury. "He's wearing you out, girl. That photo you emailed me, girl, you looked awful."

Liz was surprised by Dee Dee's need to be so brutally honest. "That is no way to talk about Stormie."

Dee Dee put her phone on speaker mode as she located the photo. "Well, I'm telling the truth."

Liz smiled warmly. "It can't be that bad."

Dee Dee glanced down at the photo on her phone. "Well, you be the judge."

"Let me open it on my phone. You are right, Dee Dee. This photo is definitely not an image of a happy bride to be."

"Thanks, you two." I really couldn't argue the point because I had been pushing myself to the limit, with all the things I needed to get done before the wedding. Their words of truth branded my soul. Both were witnesses that I needed to get my act together especially with my wedding was in August, only six months away.

"I don't know why you are marrying him!" Dee Dee's words sounded so harsh coming from her.

"Not marry Daniel?" A look of uncertainty appeared on my face as I held the telephone closer.

I dreamed about of the day Daniel would place a wedding ring on my finger as Pastor Rankin announced us as Mr. and Mrs. Daniel Booker. More than anything, I wanted a man that would tell me that we would live happily ever after. That man was Daniel.

Liz interjected, "Maybe you should at least consider postponing the wedding, Stormie."

I drew a deep breath. "I am not postponing my wedding and disappointing Daniel. He is the best thing that ever happened to me."

Dee Dee blurted out, "He treats you like dirt!"

Liz added, "I hate to admit it, but Dee Dee is right about that."

Dee Dee laughed. "I know one thing, there are only three reasons a woman stays with a man like Daniel. Either he's rich, he's good in bed, or she's crazy." She continued. "One thing for sure, he's not rich and surely don't rock her world in the bedroom. So, there is only one reason left. Girl, you're not crazy, are you?"

Liz jumped back into the conversation as she came swiftly to Stormie's defense. "You know as well as I do that she's not crazy and that she has not slept with him either."

Dee Dee chimed in. "And why not? I know I would. No way I would marry a man without finding out if he was good in bed first. This is not kindergarten and I'm not the teacher, baby."

Finally, I spoke. "Dee Dee, you are nothing but a heathen. A pure heathen."

Dee Dee burst into a session of incontrollable laughter. "Don't you go there because I remember back in the day, you couldn't keep your dress down either. Remember Michael?"

Liz giggled, officiating like a referee between us. "Oooh, she got you good with that one."

"Don't remind me. I made a fool of myself chasing behind that man. But the point is, I'm a different woman. One thing for sure, nobody else is getting me to raise it up again unless I'm married to them, period."

A ridiculing smirk ran across Dee Dee's face. "You know what your problem is, Stormie Faye Brown?"

"No, tell me what my problem is, Dee Dee Christy Taylor."

"Your problem is that you keep that mess bottled up inside you. You need a good man so you can let it out."

"Like I said, Ms. Know It All, I'm not that same woman. That woman is gone for good. I have given my life to the Lord and only to the man I marry."

"Well, tell me this, if Daniel's is not rich, you have not slept with him, and you're not crazy, why are you marrying somebody like him?

I scoffed. "What about love?"

Dee Dee's face frowned in judgement. "Girl, please, Daniel don't know the meaning of that word."

I glanced over at Daniel's picture on the night stand. I began to think about how our relationship was struggling to survive. I thought about how he wasn't even willing to talk about anything without getting mad. I quickly wiped the tears from my eyes with my hand.

"I am marrying Daniel, even if you think I shouldn't, Dee Dee. I love Daniel and he loves me. You two should be happy for me." I wiped my cheek to ward off the tears that begin to form again.

At that moment, Liz uttered her next words. "We just want the best for you. Have you talked to your Pastor about what is going on?"

I cleared my throat. "Of course, I talked to Pastor Rankin about it."

"So, what did he say about the way Daniel is treating you?"

"He told me that we needed to come for pre-martial counseling."

"Well, did you?"

"No, because Daniel said we don't need counseling. He was so upset with Pastor Rankin that he wanted to join another church but I talked him into staying. After he wouldn't go to counseling, I called Victor."

"Your stepfather, Victor? Girl, please."

"Wait Liz. I want to hear what her no good stepfather had to say."

CHAPTER TWO

Stormie

My stepfather's words came rushing back to me. "He said that, 'If you really love him, you need to prove it and tough it out. Besides, you are not getting any younger.' And he is right."

Liz carefully examined her words. "Tough it out? Even when Daniel is verbally abusive and cheated on you at least twice that you know of since you've have been engaged? C'mon."

"That's in the past. I have forgiven him for that. He promised me he wouldn't cheat on me again."

Dee Dee wrenched. "And you believed him?"

"Yes, I do. I have to trust him if I expect our relationship to work out." Anxiety stabbed me from the inside of my stomach.

Dee Dee tilted her head, eyebrows drawn. "What kind of advice is that? Your stepfather cheated on your mother more times than she could count. God bless her soul. And have you forgotten how he brought his girlfriend to your mama's funeral? That man is sick and has no morals."

Sorrow pooled inside me, right with my heart of other hidden secrets. "I remember."

I couldn't believe that I had sunken so low as to call him for his opinion about anything. As I stared out the window, my gaze fell upon a scene that unfolded on the street outside. A man and a woman were engaged in a heated argument. I didn't know them, yet something about the woman struck a chord deep within me. Her resemblance to my mother was uncanny—the same sturdy frame, the same height—although her brunette hair cascaded down her waist, a stark contrast to my mother's shoulder-length course black hair.

Seeing that couple together rekindled a captured memory of the chaos that had often surrounded my childhood. A memory of the relationship between my mother and the man who had stepped into our lives after my father passed. My stepfather's presence had brought nothing but turmoil and confusion to our family. Painful emotions that had become a familiar backdrop to my upbringing—sadness, longing, and a deep-seated desire for peace and stability.

Seeing that couple together rekindled a memory of when my stepfather's violent outbursts ruled our home. The memories rushed back, uninvited yet undeniable. I could still feel the fear that clenched my heart and the trembling in my hands as I witnessed his cruelty firsthand.

There was my stepfather holding my mother's arm with one hand as he drew back his fist and punched her face. The impact sent her sprawling to the floor, her head colliding with the unforgiving edge of the wooden coffee table. He got down on top of her and continued hitting her until she was unconscious. It was a painful memory, one that I had tried to bury deep inside me for years. I was just thankful that I was not marrying a man that was physically abusive.

I drifted slowly back when I heard Liz and Dee Dee talking.

Liz shook her head. "Dee Dee, if I had not grabbed your arm, you were going to…"

Dee Dee fisted her hand on her waist. "Shoot him? I sure was. You know I have never shot anybody with my gun, Bertha, but in his case, I was going to make an exception."

I smiled, eager to find out more about Dee's gun. "Bertha?"

Liz eased her left arm down by her side. "Yeah, the only thing she has shot with Bertha were her ex-husband's tires."

Dee Dee laughed. "That's true, girl. But I couldn't take it anymore, Liz," Dee Dee continued, her voice filled with a mixture of anger and liberation. "I followed his behind to a motel and when he and his woman went inside, I shot out all four of his tires and three of hers."

A smile stretched across Liz's face. "Only three of hers?"

Dee Dee took a deep breath with anger and satisfaction evident in her voice. "Oh, believe me, Liz, I wanted to shoot out all four of her tires, too. I couldn't let my anger consume me completely. So, I settled for three."

Stormie interjected, her voice filled with curiosity. "Dee Dee, shooting out their tires? Wasn't that extreme?"

Dee Dee shrugged, a hint of mischief in her eyes. "Maybe it was a little extreme, but at that moment, I didn't care. I wanted them to feel the hurt that he had caused me. It was my way of saying, 'You can't just go around hurting people and expect to get away with it.'"

Liz couldn't help but chuckle, her smile widening. "Dee Dee, you never cease to amaze me. I can only imagine the shock on their faces when they came out to find their tires shot out."

Dee Dee's smile grew mischievous as well. "I wish I could have seen it myself. But I was long gone before they came out of the motel room."

Liz raised an eyebrow, her tone filled with admiration. "You really showed them, Dee Dee. I can only imagine the satisfaction it must have brought you."

Dee Dee nodded, a glimmer of pride shining in her eyes. "It did bring some satisfaction, I won't lie. But now, not as much as what I did next. I rented a moving van and went by and picked up my cousins, Paul, David, and Roberto."

Liz blurted before she could stop herself. "You mean your cousin, 'Wild Dog' Roberto, the famous wrestler?"

"Yeah, that's the one. He is an expert when it comes to payback."

Liz's eyes widened with excitement as Dee Dee finally confessed the secret, she had been keeping for two years. It was hard to contain my own enthusiasm as I sensed her reaction. Liz was the biggest fan of Wild Dog, the legendary professional wrestler known for his electrifying moves and charismatic personality.

"You mean he came to your house and you didn't tell me? Girl, you know I love me some Wild

Dog. I even know his theme song. 'He's the mean-est, toughest, dog on the block. "He's Wild Dog! Wild Dog! Wild Dog! Wild Dog! Grrrrrrrrrrr…"'

Dee Dee couldn't help but chuckle at Liz's excitement over her cousin. "And you wonder why I didn't let you know. Look how you are acting. Anyway, we took everything out of the house; the furniture, curtains, my clothes, his clothes, and every picture on the wall. I mean everything."

"You know I love wrestling. Can you get me an autograph picture of him? Wild Dog! Wild Dog! Wild Dog! Grrrrrrrrrrr…"

"Alright, alright, enough about Wild Dog. Let me finish my story. My crazy cousin, Roberto, went above and beyond. He even ripped up all the carpet from the floors, broke out all the windows, and removed every last single door. He turned to me and said, 'Now, he will know how he made you feel inside, like an empty shell.'"

"I know that's right."

I even cleaned out both of our bank accounts and cancelled all the credit cards before I left town."

Liz laughed at her candidness. "You are something else. You know that Miss Goody Two-Shoes would never do that to Daniel. She is too nice. If she did leave him, she would leave him everything."

I injected taking a firm stance. "Did you two forget I'm on the phone?"

I felt a hodgepodge of emotions because my relationship with the two of them was a double-edge sword. Daniel was jealous of our friendship and my friends despised him. If they only knew him like I did, they would change their minds about him. My friends were wrong about Daniel and the thought of leaving him was terrifying. I had invested my love, time, and energy into this relationship, and I loved him despite his flaws.

Both Dee Dee and Liz wished that they could stop me from making a decision they thought that I would regret.

Dee Dee added, "Liz and I have heard how he talks down to you and how he tries to control you."

Liz's voice grew stern as she replied, "You can't keep living like that, Stormie. You deserve better than someone who treats you like that. It's not healthy."

After they realized that their cause was hopeless, they reverted back to the reason they called me in the first place.

Dee Dee, bubbled with excitement as the conversation took on a pleasant tone. "We are going on vacation to Atlanta. We want you to go with us next month!"

Liz cut in as I entertained the idea of not going. "C'mon, Stormie. It will do you good to get away. It's going to be a lot of fun."

As I reared back, I bumped my head against the headboard. I tried to cut my way out of their invitation web. "You both know how busy I am with my job, planning for the wedding, and moving my stuff into Daniel's house. There is just no way I can just drop all my plans and take a vacation with you two, right now."

Disappointment crept over Liz's face. "Didn't she promise us last year that she would go with us before she got married to you-know-who."

Dee Dee shook her head and tsk-tsked, not affected at all by my rejected answer. "Yeah, Stormie. You need this trip before you really crack up."

I shifted uneasily in the bed before I spoke. "I know you're both right but…"

Dee Dee took control of the conversation. "But nothing. This time, we are not taking no for an answer. You have almost the whole month of March to get ready for the trip."

I rubbed my forehead and stroked back my hair. "Okay, I'm going. Are you two satisfied?"

The tension around Liz's eyes eased as she issued a deep sigh. "Now since that's settled, Dee Dee, don't you have a hair appointment this morning?"

"Thanks for reminding me, girl. I sure don't want to go another week with my head looking like this."

Liz added, "And Stormie, you better get going too. It's almost six fifteen. You know how traffic is on a Monday morning."

I glanced at the clock, in a quick response. "It sure is. Bye, you two."

As I hung up the phone, I couldn't help but feel grateful for the friendship that Dee Dee, Liz, and I had cultivated over the years. We had been through everything together, from playground fights to first dates. But despite the distance and the demands of our busy lives, we always made time for each other. Our phone conversations were a lifeline; a way to stay connected and catch up on everything that was happening in each other's worlds.

I smiled as I thought about Dee Dee's upcoming hair appointment and Liz's reminder about the time. It was typical of our conversations, always a mix of lighthearted banter and practical reminders. But underneath it all was a deep sisterhood of love and support that had kept us together all these years. We were each other's cheerleaders, always there to celebrate successes and offer comfort in the difficult times.

I felt grateful for the grounding force of our friendship. No matter what challenges lay ahead, I knew that I could count on the support and love of Dee Dee and Liz. And that was a gift beyond measure.

I thought about the three of us. We were all successful, driven women who had worked hard to get where we were. But at the end of the day, we were still just three friends who loved and supported each other, no matter what.

I had just enough time to take quick shower, slip on a dress, and a pair of shoes. Hopefully, there wouldn't be an accident or heavy traffic on the freeway this morning.

CHAPTER THREE

Stormie

A year ago, Daniel proposed to me, and I received the news I had been working hard and praying for - a promotion to a Senior Financial Analyst position on Mr. Stanley's team at the corporate office of Stanley, Pierce, and Wilkerson Technologies. I couldn't believe how God had favored me. Finally, after years of dedication, hard work, and countless hours spent analyzing spreadsheets and financial reports, I was working alongside some of the most brilliant minds in the industry.

Not only was it a permanent position with benefits, but I would make ninety-six thousand dollars a year with three weeks paid vacation. It was a big increase from my salary as a temporary Financial Analyst of forty thousand dollars a year. I refused to admit it even to myself but Daniel, never thought of me as successful or intelligent in anything—just a woman who would be at his beck and call.

Still, I was determined to make this relationship work because that's what women in my family do. They learned to suffer quietly. Unlike my mother, I was never going to let a man hit me though. I meant that because I had watched my mother endure years of abuse at the hands of my stepfather. I had sworn within myself that I would never let myself become a victim.

It had been somewhat a chaotic year between my workload and planning my wedding. I loved my job. It was therapy for me. It helped me to take my mind off not only the wedding, but also Daniel. At work, I was admired, honored, and praised.

Every workday, as I walked through the grand entrance of the towering glass building that housed the corporate office, I was filled with excitement. The lobby was an impressive sight, adorned with sleek marble floors, towering pillars, and sparkling chandeliers that shimmered with a thousand points of light. The energy was palpable, with a buzz of conversation, clacking of heels, and anticipation for the day ahead.

I managed to make it to work right at seven forty-five. I didn't believe in being late, as it was something my mama had instilled in me. I rushed to my office and quickly threw my purse in the desk drawer.

I have just enough time to grab a cup of coffee. I hurried down the hall to the break room, poured a cup of hot black coffee into a clean coffee cup on the counter, and took a sip. I met several co-workers on the way back to my office. They all knew if my head and fingers waved back and forth, get out of my way, and don't try to stop me for conversation. It wasn't a time to chit-chat about who was messing around with who or who got fired. I usually didn't entertain gossip but sometimes it was just too juicy to resist. This morning, they knew the signal meant

"Don't have time, so don't tell me!" Once at my desk, I pulled the stack of file folders closer to me.

Quickly, I scanned my desk for the Lorrain Haines' project folder. I have always been very detailed-oriented, down to the last penny. As I was calculating the figures on the audit sheets, I thought to myself, *Why is this not adding up correctly?*

I began talking to the numbers, holding a one-on-one conversation with them. "There you are. Trying to hide from me. But I found you."

Mr. Justin Stanley, the president and CEO of the company, walked past my office and my conversation grabbed his attention as he stopped abruptly.

Mr. Stanley asked, "Did you find it?" The question came without judgment.

I must admit I was nervous and it showed. "Good morning, Mr. Sssstanley," I stuttered. "I hope I wasn't too loud."

Understanding flooded from his eyes. "Of course not. Other than myself, you are the only person I know, that talks to the numbers."

That was the last thing I expected to hear, considering Mr. Stanley seemed so stand-offish, even untouchable. I was so surprised to see him or even that he was actually talking to me face-to-face. Yet, he was standing right in front of my desk without his assistant or even one of his secretaries. He was considered quite the celebrity around the building because he was seldom seen.

He had started the successful engineering firm over ten years ago and held the majority of the stock. He bought out his partners years ago but keep the name the same. He owned other companies, and even real estate. Every single woman in the building had their trap set for Mr. Stanley. Why not? He was single, wealthy, and gorgeous. Most of women who worked in my department were not sure if he was African American, Porto Rican, Hispanic, or Italian. They drooled over the fact that if they married him, they would have some pretty babies. His olive complexion and thick, jet black, wavey hair didn't fool me one bit. I knew he was African American. If I had to take a guess, he was probably stood six feet six inches, and in his mid-to-late thirties. He looked more like a model that stepped off a fashion magazine cover then a successful business man. I was probably only a handful of women out of hundreds who didn't care.

I got up from my desk to at least shake his hand. He smiled as he looked down at my shoes.

A big grin broke across his face. "Are you starting a new fashion trend?"

As I glanced down at my shoes, I became aware that I was wearing one dark brown and one black shoe. I was so embarrassed. After he smiled, we both burst out into laughter. It was an ice-breaker for sure. His sense of humor broke through the cold and mysterious barriers of who I thought he was. Instead, he was warm and very personable.

"I guess I was in a hurry this morning. Not only did I wear mix matched shoes but also forgot my lunch too."

"Ms. Brown, I want to take you to lunch today. My treat."

"No, Mr. Stanley. You don't have to do that. I'll just grab a sandwich from the café."

"Meet me at twelve-thirty p.m. out front." He smiled. "Twelve-thirty p.m. out front, Ms. Brown."

"Yes, sir. Twelve-thirty p.m. out front."

Before stepping out of the door to my office, he stopped. "By the way, bring your note pad because I want to go over the Lorraine Haines' file. Do you like Italian?"

"Yes, sir, I do."

"I know this little Italian place. It's one of my favorite restaurants in the city."

For some reason, it was hard for me to look him directly in the eyes. Maybe it was my not wanting to seem too eager.

Looking down, my eyes found a comfortable place among the ceramic tiles on the floor. "Thank you and I look forward to it, sir." After completing the sentence, I looked up but he was gone.

As soon as he made his exit, my secretary, Janice Anderson rushed to the door of my office. She couldn't wait to see why Mr. Stanley made a personal visit to my office.

Janice was one was the best secretaries in the entire building. But she was nosey, suspicious, loud, and had the worst case of "man crazies" I have ever seen.

I held up my coffee cup to my lips and motioned for her to step inside. She quickly walked inside closing the door behind her. As she sat down in one of the chairs in front of my desk, I could see her right leg bobbing up and down as adrenaline rushed through her entire being.

Janice's right eyebrow arched. "What happened? Why was he in your office? Tell me every juicy detail."

"Cool down before you overheat. He just wants to discuss the Lorraine Haines' account with me over lunch that's all."

Her eyes glanced over at me with anticipation and excitement. "Over lunch? Can I go with you, please?"

"No, you can't."

"Why not? I worked on that project with you."

I released a weighty breath. "Janice, please. I don't think that typing and copying pages qualifies. Besides, I need for you to finish typing the Jenkins' report, remember?"

"Jenkins' report?"

I took a sip of coffee and leaned forward, exaggerating my point. "Yeah, Jenkins report. The one I put on your desk yesterday. I need that report before the end of the day. You better have it on my desk by five p.m."

Janice placed her hand over her mouth, giggling. "Oh, yes, right. I was just about to start on it."

"Five o'clock, Janice."

"Don't worry, I'll be finished."

"Alright, because I have enough to think about with my wedding coming up so I don't need any problems from you."

Hesitantly, she cleared her throat. "You need a wedding planner and I know the perfect one for you. But only if you tell me about lunch when you come back."

"Okay. So, what about the wedding planner?"

"Her name is Michelle Davis with *A Wedding Affair*. She is a good friend of mine and the best in town. She is usually booked two years out but I know if I call her, I can get you an appointment."

"That would be great if you can do that for me."

CHAPTER FOUR

Dee Dee

April slipped on her salon apron. She lifted up Dee Dee's hair and began to examine different sections.

"Look at these roots. You've got a hot mess up here."

"I know. Don't remind me."

"I still can't believe all this way across town just to get your hair done, girl."

"Like your slogan says, 'Not just done. DONE RIGHT. You know that you are worth the drive."

April began separating Dee Dee's hair into four sections as she used a jumbo clip to secure each one. "I know that's right. You know I appreciate your business, girl."

As April combed through a section at a time she asked, "How are you and Charles doing?"

Dee Dee laughing, "Baby, Charles is history. History!"

"Well, excuse me," said April. "He seemed like a nice guy from what you told me about him."

"Nice? Try cheap."

"Charles?"

"Yes, Charles."

"From what you told me about him, I would have never guessed he was like that."

"Me either."

April looked up from her work, intrigued. "What happened?"

"Let me tell you just how cheap he was," Dee Dee began. "He never wanted to spend money on anything. I found out just how far he's willing to go to save a buck."

April raised an eyebrow. "How far?"

"So, I was at his place, and I needed to use the restroom. I went in there, and I noticed that there was no toilet tissue," Dee Dee said, shaking her head in disbelief. "I mean, who doesn't keep toilet tissue in their bathroom?"

April chuckled. "I know, right? But go on."

"I opened the cabinet under the sink, thinking he must keep it in there. But there was nothing. And then I saw a stack of napkins in a basket from different fast-food restaurants," Dee Dee said, her voice incredulous. "I asked him about it and he told me that tissue costs too much."

April's eyes widened. "I thought he had a good job?"

Dee Dee, shaking her head. "He does and he makes good money too. He said, 'napkins were free, so why should I buy toilet tissue.'"

April shook her head as she applied the light brown hair color to Dee Dee's roots with a brush.

"That's ridiculous. You're better off without him, Dee Dee."

"Tell me about it."

"Girl, there are two things I can't stand in a man, one is a cheapskate."

Laughing, April leaned closer. "What's the other one?"

"A cheater."

April nodded in agreement. "Girl, me either."

Dee Dee leaned back against the salon chair and crossed her legs. "That's why I divorced my husband. Ain't no man going to cheat on me and get away with it."

"I wish I could get that through to my niece's hard head. I tried to tell her, if he cheats on the woman he's with, he will cheat on you, baby."

"What did she say?"

April pointed her comb toward the beige wall. "Talking to her is like me talking to that wall over there. The girl is beautiful, smart, and has a good job. She could have any man she wants."

"So is my friend, Stormie. She is smart, has a good job, and beautiful too. So, I don't get her either."

"My niece, the girl is smart when it comes to businesses but dumb as she wanna-be when it comes to men. Lately she only dates married men."

Dee Dee's eyes widened in surprise. "Why would she do that?"

April shook her head. "I don't know. She started working for this guy who's really successful in business and she got caught up in his fancy lifestyle. He was married, but he's always showered her with gifts and took her on fancy vacations. Get this, girl – he had a wife, five kids, and a dog. When his wife found out about her, she told my niece that she would track her down like a dog and shoot her. She had to come and stay with me for four months. After that close call, I hoped she learned her lesson."

"My friend and her cheating boyfriend are supposed to get married. He talks down to her and goes on these so-called "business trips" without her. I tried to tell her let that man go."

April motioned for her to walk over to the shampoo bowl. "Red flag, baby."

"Yeah, tell me about it. I even tried to tell her that if he is cheating now, when they get married it will be worse. He told her, get this, 'the reason I did it was because you won't give me any. But I won't do it again.'"

April snickered as she rinsed the hair coloring down the drain, poured on generous amount of her own formulated conditioning shampoo followed by rigorous scalp scrub. "I know how that conversation went."

"Don't you know it. She says to me, 'Dee Dee, he promised not to do it again. He is saving himself until he marries me.'"

April laughed, using a wide tooth comb to detangle and condition Dee Dee's hair. "Good luck with that."

Dee Dee tapped her left arm lightly. "Wait a minute, get this. Next thing she tells me is that she knows he is telling the truth."

They both threw their hands in the air and hollered, "Cheater!"

Dee Dee's nose wrinkled. "Yeah, you know he's just a tiger looking for his next prey."

April signaled her to come over to her chair so she could do a roller set to her hair. "She sounds just like my niece, naive when it comes to men."

"I don't play that when it comes to my man being faithful," said Dee Dee.

"Me either. You remember my stylist, Cindy Hicks, the one that had the purple hair? She worked in the second hair station over there." April pointed with the large tooth comb.

"Cindy Hicks? Yeah, I remember her. She was good at doing updos hairstyles."

"Yeah, she was good at doing more than updos."

"Really?"

April's eyes narrowed in anger. "Two weeks ago, I forgot my lunch. I had made some seafood gumbo so I decided to go home and heat up a bowl instead of stopping by that fried rice place on the corner. I love seafood gumbo. Do you like it?"

Dee Dee had been listening intently as the story reeled her in. "Love the stuff. So, what happened with Cindy?"

"Well anyway, when I opened the front door, I heard all this noise. It was coming from my bedroom. When I opened the door, my mouth almost dropped to the floor. There was my husband, James Lee and Cindy in my bed."

"What! No, he didn't?"

"Oh, yes he did and she did too."

"I knew you were beside yourself, April. I can't believe he would bring a woman to your house. That's some kind of bold. What did you do?"

"Girl, I'm telling you the truth, I couldn't move for two minutes. They were going at it so strong they didn't know I was there. I stormed to my hall closet and loaded my gun. When I came back, I started shooting. Before I could reload, the two of them jumped up and started running. I aimed for that fake purple hair on her head and his you know what. But I missed them both."

Dee Dee couldn't contain her laughter.

"Wait a minute, if you think that's funny listen to this. I shot a hole clean through the headboard of my bed. I paid over two thousand dollars for that bed. I wished I had shot him in his you know what instead of my bed. I almost cried that I ruined that headboard. I threw out the headboard, mattresses, bed frame, sheets, pillows, the rug, the dresser, the curtains hanging in the window, and burned them. You know I don't curse right?"

"Right."

"But girl, I called him every curse word I could think of and a few I made up."

Dee Dee held her stomach as the laughter poured out of her. "April, you are too much. I'm telling you-too much."

"Well, I did. But I guarantee you one thing, he won't get to do it again, at least not in that bed. I had to ask the Lord to forgive me because that was wrong, the way I cussed him out." April motioned with her hand for Dee Dee to walk over to the dryer.

"I think she had been sneaking over to my house for a while. I remember smelling women's perfume in my bedroom when I got home at night. 'Baby, you are imagining things he said.'"

Dee Dee was laughing so hard she was still holding her stomach. "Shut-up, April."

"I would catch her going through my appointment book to see if I had booked a client during my lunch time."

"Have you seen Cindy lately?"

"Seen her? Huh! She never came back to the shop to get her stuff. She had some of the most expensive high end curling irons and hair products. Probably over two thousand dollars-worth and at least a thousand dollars in products. In fact, that is what I'm using to curl your hair."

Dee Dee turned and slapped April's arm. "Get out of here, April."

"I heard she moved somewhere out of state."

"What about that husband of yours?"

"James Lee? You know me. I'm just too forgiving. He begged me until I took him back but I told him next time, I'm not going to miss. So, if I was him, I would keep my pants zipped and his choo choo train at the station until I buy a ticket to ride."

Laughter rushed past Dee Dee's lips. "My ex-husband was different. He'll stop messing around for a while, then he'd start-up again. He couldn't handle what he had at home but he was sneaking around like a cat in heat. My new boyfriend, Gerald, is not like him or Charles at all, girl."

"New boyfriend? April questioned as she turned on the hair dryer for it to start heating up.

"You heard right. And girl, that man is fine. He's so fine that if you looked up the word fine online, his name would be there."

April slapped Dee Dee on her back. "Hush your mouth, girl."

A smile rang across Dee Dee's face. "That man is God sent. He goes to church, has own business, never been married, no children, and that man loves him some Dee Dee."

April gave a slight chuckle as she cleaned out the shampoo bowl and placed the wet towels into the hamper. "Should I pray for you?"

A mischievous smile spread across Dee Dee's face as her eyes widened. "No, pray for him. He already told me that he doesn't believe in sleeping around. But we'll see about that."

Laughter burst forth from inside of April. "You better behave yourself then."

Dee Dee giggled. "I don't even know the meaning of those words."

"I heard you, girl. I'm happy for you because you deserve a good man. Do you need a magazine to read while you're under the dryer?"

Dee Dee pushed to the back of the seat, pointing towards countertop, "Yeah, hand me that magazine on top with the latest hair styles."

CHAPTER FIVE

Stormie

I had just finished calculating the cost and writing the evaluation of the Lorraine Haines project at twelve fifteen. I grabbed my black purse from the desk drawer and hand full of pencils and threw them inside. I picked up the Lorraine Haines project folder put it in my briefcase as I rushed towards the elevator.

Once I made my way to the lobby, there was Mr. Stanley's personal assistant, Jeff Barley. Jeff had a sort of a starchy personality. Always on top of his game. I guess he had to be to handle the demands of Mr. Stanley's schedule. In fact, it was Jeff who interviewed me for my position.

"Good afternoon, Ms. Brown. Mr. Stanley is waiting for you out front."

"Thank you, Jeff."

Out of the corner of my eye, I could see Jeff following me from behind. I was shocked as I headed out the door. There was Mr. Stanley in the front seat of a black Porsche Panamera, waving for me to get in. Mr. Stanley never drove. He always arrived by limousine and was ushered to his office by one of his secretaries, Jeff, or others I didn't know.

"From the look on your face, you are surprised that I am driving, aren't you?" questioned Mr. Stanley as he took off his shades and held them in his hand.

"Well, I didn't know for sure if you knew how."

Jeff opened the car door as I took a seat inside. Then, Mr. Stanley placed his shades back over his eyes. Jeff barely had time to close the door before Mr. Stanley sped off. I quickly fastened my seat belt as he whisked me away.

When we arrived at the restaurant, a valet opened my door and reached for my hand to help me out of the car. Mr. Stanley handed him the keys. I could see in the valet's hand a corner of a fifty-dollar bill which accompanied the keys.

"Thanks, Matt."

Mr. Stanley walked in favor because we didn't have to even wait on a table or stand in line. Every few minutes, Mr. Stanley would bring up in the conversation about my shoes and we both would laugh about it. He pointed it out to the hostess at the restaurant, the waiter, and a few other customers who walked by. He had such a refreshing sense of humor. I hate to admit it but I loved it.

I observed Mr. Stanley across the table, his eyes sparkling with enthusiasm as his eyes scanned the menu. With each turn of the page, he discussed the various dishes that were his preferences. The pages unfolded before us like a treasure trove of culinary delights. As my fingers traced the words, my choices began to take shape. Finally, after careful consideration and with an air of excitement, I made my decision. Mr. Stanley's favorite, a perfectly cooked pasta drenched in a rich tomato sauce, stole the spotlight, capturing his attention and bringing a smile to his face. I, too, was drawn to my selection—a delectable risotto infused with fragrant herbs and creamy parmesan cheese.

As I closed the menu, my taste buds were already tingling in anticipation of the dish that would arrive. As the waiter approached our table, we eagerly placed our orders. The waiter nodded with a knowing smile, recognizing our eagerness to indulge in the authentic flavors that awaited us. With a graceful bow, he retreated to the bustling kitchen.

Midway through our meal, Mr. Stanley lifted his gaze from his plate and locked eyes with me, his expression sincere and appreciative. "I want to commend you on all the projects you have worked on," his voice filled with admiration. "You truly have a remarkable ability to work wonders with the numbers."

A warm smile spread across my face as I accepted his kind words. The recognition from the President and CEO meant a great deal to me, affirming the dedication and expertise I had poured into my work. It was a gratifying moment, a validation of my skills and contributions to the company.

"Thank you, Mr. Stanley. This food is absolutely delicious," I expressed with genuine satisfaction. The flavors lingered on my palate, reminding me of the joy that comes with indulging in authentic Italian cuisine.

As we finished our meal, Mr. Stanley suggested we take the scenic route back to the office, allowing for more time to chat. I eagerly agreed, intrigued by the unexpected connection we seemed to share. During the drive, we discovered shared interests, from hobbies to favorite books and movies. We exchanged stories and laughter, each moment strengthening our bond.

I couldn't help but feel a genuine connection with Mr. Stanley, appreciating his easygoing nature and the sense of camaraderie that had developed between us.

As he pulled into the office parking lot, I couldn't help but reflect on the surprising turn of events. I had never imagined developing such a rapport with my boss. It felt refreshing to have someone at work with whom I could connect on a personal level. Although I valued the professional relationship I had with Mr. Stanley, I couldn't deny the spark of friendship that had ignited during our lunch and drive. I realized that sometimes, unexpected connections could bring joy and fulfillment to my everyday life.

With a newfound sense of excitement and optimism, I stepped out of the car, ready to continue my workday. I couldn't help but look forward to future conversations and shared experiences with Mr. Stanley.

I found myself drawn to Mr. Stanley's easygoing nature and his ability to make me feel at ease. The exchange felt effortless and genuine, as if we had known each other for far longer than our professional relationship would suggest. It was a rare and delightful connection that left me feeling grateful for the opportunity to engage with such an insightful individual. I found him to be quite charming and a gentleman. A rare gift, even in my own fiancé.

As we entered the building, Mr. Stanley turned to me and said, "You know, I've been thinking about promoting you to head the Finance Department after Mrs. Crawford retires next year. Your work has been exceptional, and I think you make a perfect fit."

I was taken aback by his words. I never expected to hear something like that from anyone, let alone from the company's President and CEO. My heart raced with excitement as I thanked him for his consideration.

From that day forward, my relationship with Mr. Stanley changed. He became more than just a boss, but a mentor and friend.

CHAPTER SIX

Dee Dee

April handed Dee Dee a mirror as she removed the cape from around her shoulders.

Dee Dee gave April a satisfied smile as she stood to her feet adjusting her dress. "Girl, I look gorgeous. I am glad you could work me in. I have a date with Gerald Saturday night. He's taking me to a steakhouse, Briscoe's."

"That place is very expensive."

Dee Dee took out her phone to send a payment to April's account. "I know. How much do I owe you?"

"The same as last time."

"Okay, done."

The two exchanged hugs as April booked her another appointment in four weeks. The door clicked as Dee Dee got into her car and backed out as she heard the crunching of the gravel in the parking lot. Another car pulled right into the indented tire tracks she left behind.

Britney

April fixed her eyes on the tall six-foot figure that graced the door. Her mouth tightened as she crossed her arms, "Britney, you're late. Of all days to be late, why did you pick this day? And you know I'm short one stylist."

Britney made a dash for her salon chair making herself comfortable. "I know but it wasn't my fault, Aunt April. My flight was late getting in."

April's eyebrow raised. "You always got an excuse, don't you? You could have at least called to let me know."

Breaking away from April's stern gaze she nodded in agreement. "You're right. You're right, I should have called. But all you have to do is give me a quick wash, blow dry, and flat iron my hair. Come on, you know I am your favorite niece."

The words soothed April's upset tone as it vanished away. She picked up a detailing comb and began to rake it through her hair. "You better be glad that you're not just my favorite but my only niece. I couldn't put up with more than one of you. How is your job going?"

"Auntie, I love it. I am on the go most of the time. I get to fly all over the world and meet new people."

"So, what do you do?"

"I buy businesses for my company and sell them at a profit to other companies. Mostly entertainment businesses, hotels, and restaurants.

"Being on the go all the time, I bet you don't have much time for romance anymore."

"You are wrong about that because I have a date Saturday night. That's why I can't be looking any kind of way. I finally found my soulmate. I'm telling you, Auntie."

April rolled her eyes and shook her head. "Britney, please."

"I know I have said that before, Auntie. But this time I mean it."

"Soulmate, huh? Well, how long have you known this one?"

"Two months."

"Two months? Please. You can't find out if that's his real hair color in two months. And you think he's your soulmate? Lean back so I can wash your hair."

"I know. I do not believe it myself. I am telling you, Auntie. I am hearing wedding bells."

April scrutinized her. "You are only twenty-two years old and I know you. You are not ready to settle down. How many times have you heard wedding bells in the last two years? Four times, Britney. Four times. This man is no different than the one you were in love with six months ago."

Britney drew a deep breath. "You're wrong this time, Auntie. He is the one."

"So, where did you meet this man?"

"I met him in New York. I had just got off the plane when I realized that I had misplaced my cell phone and he was kind enough to let me use his phone to call a taxi. And guess what?"

"What?"

"As I was checking into the hotel, someone tapped me on the shoulder. When I turned around, it was him. We both had booked a room at the same hotel. Can you believe it?"

"No, but go on."

"He invited me to have a drink with him later that evening. We have so much in common that we talked practically all night."

"Knowing you, there's more to this story."

"How did you know? He invited me to dinner the next night. Before I knew, we were in bed together. And let me tell you that it was incre-d-ible."

April stomach recoiled. "How did that happen?"

"I don't know. It just happened."

"Britney, sleeping with a person don't just happen. I thought you said you were not going to mess around anymore until you got married?"

April snickered with delight. "That's not the shameful part. He's engaged to be married."

"Britney, you have lost your cotton-picking mind! I don't believe you. You mean to tell me that you are sleeping around with an engaged man?"

"So, what's the problem? He's not married yet."

"Let me get this straight. You meet single men all over the world, but you are messing around with a man that is about to be married? As pretty as you are, you can have any single man you want."

"Don't worry, Auntie. I know that eventually, he is going to break up with her then we can get married. So, what's the problem?"

"The problem is he's just playing you. I wish I could get through to that thick head of yours, if he cheats on his fiancé, what makes you think that he won't cheat on you? Don't you get it? As far as he is concerned, you are just the other woman."

Britney held her hands to her face shielding it from the heat of the blow dryer.

"He does not love her. He said that since he met me, he realized that the only reason he is marrying her is because she is pressuring him."

April paused, her eyes widened with concern. "And you believed him? What if he gets you get pregnant? You risk throwing your career out the window."

"I am smart enough not to let that happen."

April responded. "Okay, Missy. Just don't expect me to babysit."

"Auntie, you are too funny."

April pulled out a flat iron from under the counter behind her and turned it to a high setting. "What if his fiancé finds out about you?"

A wide grin took shape on Britney's face as she ignored the fact that her aunt could be right. "He loves me. That's all I care about. He's taking me to dinner at this fancy steakhouse."

Just as April had curled the last section of her hair, the door of the salon swung open. Two additional clients stepped inside and their conversation came to an abrupt ending.

Stormie

I stood at my office door and hesitated before I entered. I knew it wouldn't be long before Janice would come running down the hall once she heard my door close. I pulled out my desk chair and took a seat. A chuckle began to stir inside of me when I heard fast paced footsteps coming closer and closer to the door.

Curiosity nibbled at Janice to the point that she rushed inside and closed the door, "How was lunch?"

"It was nice." I refused to give her any details for her imagination to run wild as I was gazing out the window and watched the trees sway in the breeze.

"And where did he take you for lunch?"

We went to Rocco's Italian Restaurant."

"Did he try to kiss you or anything romantic?"

"Of course, not? He was a perfect gentleman. If he had, I would have set him straight. You know that I'm engaged. Like I told you, it was a business lunch."

"And?" Janice prodded.

"And what?"

Janice's eyes widened. "Is he available?"

I smiled and played it cool. "I don't know. I didn't ask him about his personal life. Like I told you, it was a business luncheon. Besides, he is not your type."

Janice's eyes lowered as she placed a file on my desk. "He's rich, handsome, and single. That's sounds like my type to me."

"You need to get your mind off of Mr. Stanley and on the Jenkins report."

Janice giggled, holding up her right hand. "I pledge that once we are married, I promise to focus on my work."

"What about the Jenkins report?"

Janice handed me a file folder. "And here is the Jenkins report. Oh, by the way, my friend, Michelle, the wedding planner, had a last-minute cancellation. I scheduled you for an appointment with her at six on Thursday evening."

The news was so welcome knowing that my life would become less hectic if I didn't have to figure out the formula to a successful wedding day.

"Janice, you are the greatest."

Janice grinned. "I know." She closed the door and made her way back to the receptionist area.

Despite my persistent attempts, I had been unable to reach Daniel Monday evening nor the entire day on Tuesday or Wednesday. I desperately sought confirmation from him about meeting with Michelle. There was no response, leaving me feeling increasingly frustrated and perplexed. The absence of any response from Daniel only fueled my growing frustration and confusion. It was disheartening to be left hanging, wondering why he had chosen to ignore me during such a crucial moment. The questions swirled in my mind, taunting me with their unanswered presence. *Why was he silent when he knew just how important this was to me?*

With mounting anxiety, the clock ticked closer to six p.m. on Thursday. It was precisely at five fifty-five just five minutes before the scheduled appointment, that Daniel finally responded.

Text: "I'm busy. You handle it."

The text struck me like a sharp blow, and my heart sank. It felt like a deflation of hope, leaving me both hurt and disappointed.

Shaking off my emotions, a voice greeted me as I rushed inside the beautifully decorated reception area of the building. Michelle Davis was waiting in the lobby and escorted me to a spacious conference room with a large oak conference table covered with several overstuffed wedding books and magazines.

As we settled into the chairs, Michelle kindly offered me a drink. I politely declined as my mind was preoccupied with the absence of Daniel by my side. The weight of his absence loomed over the conversation, unspoken but palpable.

"Ms. Brown, I am so glad to finally meet you," Michelle began, her tone professional yet empathetic. "What time will your fiancé be joining us?" Her she inquired, her curiosity tinged with a hint of concern.

Raising an eyebrow, I hoped to convey my willingness to proceed without delving into the intricacies of my personal life. "His schedule is incredibly busy at the moment. Unfortunately, he won't be able to make it." I attempted to maintain a composed demeanor despite the disappointment and frustration simmering within.

Michelle nodded understandingly, her gaze filled with empathy. It was clear that she had encountered similar situations before, where a partner's absence in wedding planning discussions presented its own set of challenges.

"Well, Ms. Brown, let's get started." Michelle shifted the focus back to the matter at hand. "I have some ideas and options to share with you. Together, we'll create a beautiful and memorable wedding day."

In that moment, I resolved to push past the disappointment and embrace the opportunity to work closely with Michelle. Although Daniel's absence stung, I wouldn't allow it to dampen my determination to create a wedding that reflected our love and commitment.

Michelle hesitated as if debating what her next words would be. "Usually, it's helpful to have the groom here but I'm sure we can manage. With my expertise and your vision, I know that we can plan a day that would be truly special. Tell me about your wedding date, your budget, and what you would like for us to help you with."

"I only have less than six months before the wedding. I need help with everything. My budget is twenty-five thousand dollars so I hope that is enough."

"We can do a lot with that amount."

Michelle took out her calculator, note pad, and a pen from her briefcase. With her swift fingers, she started adding up the prices as she wrote down a list. The venue, photographer, catering, and drinks.

"Non-alcoholic drinks please."

"Yes, of course. Non-alcoholic drinks, flowers, decorations, wedding and groom cake, rehearsal dinner, reception DJ, food, gifts for the wedding party, and limo service to and from the venues. What about the minister?"

"My Pastor, Pastor Rankin, will perform the ceremony." I handed his business card to her. "Here is his contact information."

"Do you have a photo of you and your fiancé. We will put up a bridal page and a gift registry. You will need to go through and select the gifts you would like from each store and the address you would like the gifts shipped to."

"That's wonderful." I pulled out my phone and texted her a photo of Daniel and me.

After Michelle saw us together, she gave me a cursory glance as she focused on the photo. "This is your fiancé?"

"Yes, that's him, Daniel Booker, the love of my life."

As moments passed and Michelle concentrated on the photo, her determined gaze hinted at a memory struggling to resurface. The intensity of her search was evident as she delved into the depths of her recollection. "I have seen him before. I never forget a face," she recounted. Her tone filled with a mix of curiosity and determination.

I offered a possible explanation, attempting to shed light on Daniel's frequent travels. "Well, he travels a lot because of his job," hoping it would provide some context for Michelle's recollection.

She pondered the idea, considering the similarities in their travel experiences. "Maybe that's where I've seen him. I do travel extensively too," Michelle suggested, her words sparking a realization within me.

Her comment caused me to reflect on how my own life had shifted after I started dating Daniel. The once frequent adventures and travels with Dee Dee and Liz had become scarce as my focus shifted towards building a life with him.

"Let me get you a total."

"I'm hoping that I am not over budget."

Michelle smiled politely. "No, you are just under your budget. Everything comes to twenty-four thousand, three hundred dollars."

I was relieved by her response.

"Your down payment is twenty percent and the balance due in two weeks before your wedding. Will you be paying the down payment by check or credit card?"

CHAPTER SEVEN

Stormie

The sun was gracefully descending on the horizon, casting a warm golden glow over the neighborhood. The cool breeze of a beautiful Friday evening filled the air, gently rustling the leaves of nearby trees as I busily made final preparations for grilling chicken fajitas outside. The tantalizing aroma of marinated chicken wafted through the backyard, intermingling with the scent of fragrant herbs and spices, promising a mouthwatering feast ahead.

I could hear the doorbell chiming, its sound carrying a sense of urgency. Uncertain of what awaited me at the front door, I took a deep breath, wiping my hands on a kitchen towel as I made my way inside to face whatever awaited me on the other side. The persistent doorbell rings and subsequent knocks reverberated through the entryway, momentarily startling me. Curiosity mingled with apprehension as I cautiously approached the door, peering through the sheer curtains that adorned the right-side panel of the front door.

Daniel stood at the front door, his eagerness to get inside evident in his restless demeanor, seeking shelter from the cool night air. Confusion mingled with cluttered emotions as I recalled his refusal to answer my calls and the deafening silence that followed my unanswered text messages throughout Thursday.

Both relief and anger pulsed through my veins, leaving me uncertain whether I should even grant entrance to the man I was about to marry. I couldn't help but express my frustration, questioning his lack of communication and absence at the appointment with the wedding planner. Questions danced on the tip of my tongue, desperate for answers, as

I hesitated at the threshold. The defensiveness tone in my voice surprised him. Not just him, it even surprised me. "Why haven't you returned my calls?"

Guilt flickered across Daniel's face, a fleeting recognition of his actions. He averted his gaze, unwilling to meet my eyes directly, as if struggling to find the right words.

"It won't happen again. I promise," he murmured, his voice laced with remorse.

Usually, those words would melt my heart so fast that they would overpower my mind releasing a surge of forgiveness. When he said them tonight, they didn't penetrate me as he stepped inside the doorway.

A soft tone came from his lips. "What's for dinner tonight?"

"I wasn't expecting you."

"I'm sure you can find something."

My heart softened as he slipped his hands around my waist, pulling me closer to him followed by a kiss. My hard exterior peeled away before he let me go.

"I'm making me some chicken fajitas."

He stroked my arm. "I know you can make enough for the both of us."

As I carefully put more chicken on the grill, Daniel's self-centeredness became evident through his words. He couldn't help but boast about his accomplishments and how others at work were constantly praising him. While his ego grew, I focused on setting the table, arranging the plates, tortillas, and an assortment of delicious toppings for the fajitas. Although he just dropped by unannounced, I was still glad to see him.

As I plated the sizzling chicken fajitas and placed them on the table, Daniel's preoccupation with himself persisted. His constant need for validation and recognition overshadowed the evening.

"You left the chicken on the grill too long," he remarked, his mouth full as he spoke. "And you really don't need to use so much salt. These tortillas taste old."

Though I had put my heart into preparing the meal, his comments chipped away at my confidence. I tried to brush off his negativity, desperately hoping the rest of the evening would improve.

Daniel's focus remained solely on himself and the accolades he received from his colleagues. I sighed, trying to maintain composure, hoping that perhaps his self-centeredness would dissipate as the evening progressed. However, deep down, I couldn't help but feel a tinge of disappointment that Daniel's own success seemed to overshadow the simple joy of our shared meal.

Daniel's constant criticism took away from my efforts. I had hoped for a pleasant evening together, but his comments only served to dampen the mood.

The silence grew heavy, only interrupted by the sound of utensils scraping against plates. I decided to speak up, voicing my concerns in a calm but firm tone. Yet, anxiety swept over me as I carefully and cautiously considered my words. "I got a call from Dee Dee the other day."

Daniel stopped eating. His brows lifted as he paused and stared straight at me. "Every single time that woman calls, she gives you bad advice. You're stupid enough to follow it. She's nothing but a troublemaker."

"Please don't call her that. She's my friend and you know it."

I looked into his light brown eyes that were now filled with anger. "What did she want anyway?"

I gave him a faint smile as I started clearing the dishes from the table. "She wants me to go on a vacation with her and Liz to Atlanta next month."

Daniel's eyes and his voice became inquisitive. "Atlanta?"

"Yes, Atlanta."

He sat up straight up in his chair and cleared his throat. "If anybody needs a vacation it's me. I don't know why you think you need one. All you do at work is run your mouth on the telephone and drink coffee all day. That's not a real job."

"That's not fair, Daniel. I do have a real job."

He folded his hands in defiance. "Huh! Real job my foot."

"I can't believe you said that. One of the reasons I qualified for my job was because I have a Bachelor's Degree in Finance."

"Well, Ms. Stormie Brown, you wasted your money even going to college. A person without a degree could do your job."

As I looked at him, I tried not to let those words penetrate my heart but it was too late. They went in like a bullet fired at close range. The more he talked, the more pain I felt inside of my soul.

Jealously is cruel in any form. For Daniel, jealously had become his partner that conspired against me. One that wounded me often and showed no mercy. When I started making more money than Daniel was when he really started acting different towards with me. I knew it was because of his ego. He was jealous of me and felt like I was competing with him. I had no idea that it would create so much tension between us.

"Look Stormie, you're my fiancé, and I wish you'd start acting like one." His voice rose again. "You're not going. Do you hear me?"

I had to force myself to say it without stuttering. "I'm going to Atlanta."

Daniel's eyes bucked wide open. My bold response took him by surprise. "What did you say?"

My voice rose with courage. "I said that I'm going."

He fastened his eyes on me again as he balled up his hand and hit the table.

I flinched.

He pushed his chair back from the table, stood up, and drew back his hand ready to strike me but he felt the vibration of his cell phone in his pocket. He took out his phone from his pants pocket, looking at the number. "I'm done, end of story. You're not going!"

He stormed outside, slamming the door behind him.

I slowly tiptoed towards where he was standing with his back to the window. I opened the window slightly.

As he answered the phone he said, "Yeah, what's up? I'm alright. Just upset. Yeah, who else?"

His anger turned into laughter. "I know that's right. You always do."

Daniel knew how to put on a good show, especially in front of the ladies at church and when we were out in public. He knew how to play the role that he was the most kind, affectionate, and loving person anyone would ever meet. If only people knew the extent of his verbal abuse towards me, they wouldn't believe it. I found myself willingly turning a blind eye, convinced that his love for me eclipsed the pain he inflicted.

I pressed my ear against the window seal even harder until it began to burn. His voice faded out as he headed for his car and drove off. My heart felt like it sunk in my stomach. *Where was he headed to? Was it to the arms of another woman?*

My mind raced with a mix of fear, doubt, and a resolute determination not to let history repeat itself. I took a deep breath, trying to calm the rising storm of emotions within me. I reminded myself that I had chosen to forgive Daniel for his past transgressions. I felt guilty for even thinking that he was cheating on me. I promised him that I had forgiven him and now I just needed to trust him and stop letting my imagination run away with me. I refused to believe that about him now.

I stood firm in my refusal to believe that Daniel would betray my trust again. But as the reality sank in that Daniel might be unfaithful, I couldn't help but draw a parallel to my mother's situation. The thought of enduring the pain and heartbreak my mother had experienced with my stepfather was unbearable. I remembered the love and commitment she had for my stepfather, despite his infidelity. I was determined to break the cycle and not let a man cheat on me, repeating the mistakes of the past.

The knowledge of my mother's own struggles with infidelity, abuse, and the toll it took on her heart weighed heavily on my own journey. I had witnessed the tears, the sleepless nights, and the moments of despair etched into her face. Now, I found myself sailing in waters she had already traveled, facing the same questions and doubts that plagued her. In those moments, it felt like destiny had tied our stories together, reminding me of the interconnectedness of our lives. The pain and scars that marked my mother's past were now etched into my own. It had always puzzled me, but now, when I faced the similar situation, I began to understand.

Love had a way of blurring my judgment of what was right and wrong. It made me hold on to hope and see the best in Daniel, even when faced with evidence of his betrayal. It was that same love that kept my mother by my stepfather's side, hoping for change and clinging to the belief that their relationship was worth fighting for.

In a strange and twisted way, it all made sense to me now. Love and commitment are powerful forces, causing me to endure the unthinkable. I realized that my love for Daniel had clouded my judgment and made me willing to forgive and give him another chance, just like my mother had done. With a mix of emotions swirling inside me, it reminded me that love can be both a source of strength and vulnerability.

It took me over an hour to pull myself together. I couldn't believe it but he almost hit me. I couldn't get it out of my mind. I sat down in the overstuffed blue suede chair next to the window and cried.

CHAPTER EIGHT

Britney

Britney walked into the dimly lit the Briscoe Steakhouse. The restaurant was packed as it usually was on a Saturday night. She had barely made it to the hostess booth when a voice called out to her.

"Over here," a familiar voice directed her to an intimate booth tucked away in the corner. It was perfect for a romantic evening. As she searched the restaurant with her eyes, she spotted him waiting for her. A big smile came upon his face as she made her way over to the table where he was sitting.

Daniel grabbed her hand and pulled her down into the seat next to him. "You're late, young lady. It's almost eight o'clock."

He kissed her on her lips and placed his arm around her waist pulling her closer to him.

"I know but I just got in. My flight was late. There was a storm coming out of Virginia. You know how much I hate flying when there is turbulence. Have you ordered yet?"

"Of course, and it should be coming out soon."

"Good. I am starving."

"Why didn't you call me when you got in? You know I worry about you."

Uncertainty brewed inside her at his response. "I know you won't believe it but I lost my cell phone."

"Again? What is it now, your fifth phone you've lost this year?"

Sarcastically, she responded, "No, it's my third but who's counting?"

He smiled. "I am. Where do you think you left it?"

"I don't know. After I talked to you last night, I might have left it at the airport."

"Baby, you lose your phone more than anybody I know. It's that job of yours. It's stressing you out."

"Stop it, Daniel. You know that my job has nothing to do with it."

He continued as he kissed her on her neck. As Britney glanced around the restaurant, she noticed the way people were looking at them—some with disapproval, others with pity. She felt a wave of guilt wash over her. Did they know he was engaged to someone else? Or was it because she was much younger than him?

As they waited for their food, Britney couldn't help but feel a sense of unease. She knew what they were doing was wrong, but she couldn't resist the thrill of being with Daniel. He had promised her the world and she had fallen for his lies. But now, sitting in a fancy restaurant with him, surrounded by disapproving looks from other diners, she felt a pang of regret.

"Are you okay?" Daniel asked, noticing the change in her demeanor.

Britney nodded, forcing a smile. "Yeah, I'm fine. Just a little nervous, I guess."

Daniel leaned in closer, placing a hand on her thigh. "Don't worry, baby. Everything is going to be okay. You know that Big Daddy is going to take care of you, right?"

She knew that Daniel was engaged but she was not just the other woman like her Aunt April had told her.

He was charming, handsome, and had a way of making her feel special. There was something about the way he looked at her like she was the only person in the world that mattered to him. She was half his age and that made her feel secure at times.

The server held up their order on a large silver tray as it rested on the back of his hand. Bring attention to himself, he cleared his throat. "Huh hum."

Daniel leaned away slightly from Britney as the server placed the plates and drinks on the table.

"Is there anything else I can do for you, sir?" Cutting his eyes towards Britney.

"No, everything looks good." He turned his attention back to Britney.

Britney's appetite dwindled as her thoughts fixated on the weighty words imparted by her auntie. In that moment, the seeds of guilt sprouted within the stony soil of her heart, their tender shoots stretching towards her conscience. She couldn't escape the overwhelming sense of guilt for her involvement in Daniel's infidelity. Deep down, she knew their actions were morally wrong, but the intoxicating chemistry between them was undeniable. Despite the guilt gnawing at her, she found herself entangled in a web of emotions too strong to resist.

She pushed her food around her plate, lost in thought. She wondered, *What Daniel's fiancé would think if she knew he was here with her. Would she be heartbroken? Angry? Would she confront him, would she fight her, or would she quietly walk away?*

Daniel placed his hand on her thigh to distract her thoughts. "So, when is your next flight?"

"I have to fly out to New York next week."

"I wish you would quit that job and find something local."

Britney blew out a hearty breath. "Daniel, please don't start that again."

"I thought you wanted to spend more time with me?"

"I do. You know that."

His fingers ran through the bouncing curls in her shoulder length brown hair. "Then, prove it. Quit."

"Like I told you before, I'm not quitting my job."

"You can come and work for me. I could use someone with your skills on my team."

Britney raised her eyebrows in surprise. "Work for you?"

Britney hesitated, unsure of how to respond. She knew that working for Daniel would be a bad idea, especially given their complicated relationship. But the thought of spending more time with him was tempting. "I don't know, Daniel. That's a big decision."

He leaned in closer to her. "Think about it."

Britney felt her heart race as she looked into his eyes. She knew that their relationship was a dangerous game they were playing, but she couldn't resist him.

"I'll think about it," she finally said, her voice barely above a whisper.

Daniel smiled. "Good. That's all I ask. Well, at least we get to spend an entire week together next month without her interrupting our plans. She is going to Atlanta."

As Daniel glanced up, he saw two figures entering the restaurant. Dee Dee and her boyfriend unexpectedly standing at the hostess desk. He did a double-take then his eyes bucked. "Ah, man. What is she doing here?"

"Who?"

"Stormie's friend, Dee Dee and her boyfriend."

Fearing the consequences of being caught, Daniel's mind raced, desperately formulating a plan to make a discreet exit without arousing suspicion from Dee Dee or the man accompanying her. Daniel could feel his heart pounding under his shirt, aware that his entire future hinged on avoiding detection. The impending engagement hung heavy in the air, as any misstep could shatter the fragile trust he had regained from Stormie.

He quickly pulled out two hundred-dollar bills from his wallet. Taking Britney's hand, he motioned with his head for the waiter and as he stood up, he placed the money in his hand.

"Let's get out of here."

Daniel's sudden gesture of giving the waiter an extra hundred dollars made Britney feel even uneasy and cheap.

As they walked out of the restaurant, Daniel glanced back over his shoulder to see if Dee or her boyfriend spotted them. He breathed a sigh of relief when he saw that they were nowhere in sight.

The car ride to the hotel was filled with an uncomfortable silence. Britney couldn't shake off the feeling of uneasiness that lingered after the restaurant incident. She looked out of the window, watching the city lights pass by, hoping to distract herself from the turmoil within. Finally, unable to bear the silence any longer, she turned to Daniel.

"Babe, we need to talk about what happened back there," she said, her voice trembling slightly.

Daniel glanced at her, his face showing a mixture of guilt and cowardness. "I know, Britney. I messed up," he admitted, his voice filled with remorse. "I didn't handle the situation well and I'm sorry if I made you feel uncomfortable."

Britney nodded, grateful that he acknowledged his mistake. "It's just... I never expected something like that from you. It made me question everything," she confessed, her voice barely above a whisper.

Daniel sighed, his grip on the steering wheel tightened. "I understand, Britney. But I want you to know that I care about you and I never intended to hurt you."

As they pulled up to the hotel parking lot, Britney took a deep breath and tried to push the event out of her mind.

"Did you bribe the waiter at the restaurant to keep quiet about us?" Britney asked, her voice shaking with worry.

"No, I just want to make sure that he was compensated for his trouble that's all," Daniel replied, trying to sound nonchalant. In reality, he was just as nervous as Britney about getting caught.

"Why did you give the waiter extra money? Were you trying to bribe him or something?"

Daniel's expression changed and he looked at her with a mix of anger and frustration. "Don't ruin this evening for me please! I get enough of that from Stormie."

As Daniel's lips formed the name "Stormie," the sound reverberated in the air, instantly triggering a storm of emotions within April. It was the first time she had heard Stormie's name spoken in her presence, and it felt like a sudden intrusion upon their private, intimate moment. A whirlwind of thoughts and doubts consumed Britney's mind as she grappled with the implications of that utterance.

Why, she wondered, *would Daniel choose this moment to mention her name, Stormie? What did it*

mean for their relationship, their connection? Storm-
ie's name carried with it a weight of reality, making
their affair feel more substantial, more tangible, and
yet, simultaneously, more illicit. Britney couldn't
help but question her place in Daniel's life, her
significance in comparison to Stormie. In the midst
of the swirling emotions, Britney found herself torn
between longing and hesitation, desire and doubt.

As Britney sat in the lobby while Daniel
checked into the hotel, she couldn't help but feel
uneasy about their conversation. The way Daniel
had brushed off her concerns and avoided eye
contact when she questioned his overly generous
tip to the waiter raised doubts in her mind. It was as
if he was hiding something, deflecting her curiosity
with half-truths and evasive answers. The realization hit her like a wave crashing against the shore.
If Daniel was capable of deceiving her about something as seemingly insignificant as a tip, what else
had he lied about? A rush of uncertainty coursed
through her veins, as she fought to maintain her
composure, unwilling to let her emotions spiral
out of control.

While riding in the hotel elevator, he grabbed her around the waist and kissed her several times passionately on her neck. As they entered the hotel room, Daniel took her in his arms and whispered into her ear, making her feel desired and wanted. She gave in to her desires pushing away the guilt and focused on the moment.

CHAPTER NINE

Stormie

As I continued driving, the rain started to come down harder. The traffic seemed to be moving even slower than before and I was starting to feel anxious. It was another Monday morning. I wasn't sure if there was a traffic accident or a stalled car ahead. I could barely see the car in front of me. As I approached a bend in the road, I saw a line of brake lights ahead of me. The traffic had come to a complete stop. I let out a sigh of frustration and checked the time—five-thirty am.

My phone rang through the car speakers. I pushed the talk button on the steering wheel to talk.

Moments passed before Liz spoke. "Hey, Stormie, I called your house but you didn't answer."

"Yeah, sorry about that. I had to leave earlier than usual," I replied, trying to keep my focus on the road.

Dee Dee's voice chimed in from the background. "Hey, Stormie. Why did you leave so early?"

"Just trying to finish up several big projects before our vacation and my secretary is coming over after work with her truck to help me move some of my things to Daniel's house. She's a blessing."

Liz let out a small sigh. "Sounds like you've got a busy day ahead of you just like me."

"Yeah, it's been a bit hectic," I said, trying to brush off the feeling of guilt of going on vacation without Daniel's approval that was gnawing at me.

Liz sipped from her coffee mug before she used her computer to log in to look at the flight schedule for the month.

"That's why I had to leave earlier." I turned on the blinkers for a lane change.

Dee Dee's bright brown eyes widened as she sat down in one of her tan leather living room chairs. "The sun is not even up yet."

Liz continued as she scrolled down the computer screen then paused.

Dee Dee chimed in. "Yeah, two hours early? Come on, what's up with that?"

"Nothing is up. I'm trying to finish up a project. And my boss is taking me to lunch again."

Liz shook her head. "Again? Didn't he take you out last week?"

"Yeah, and…?"

Dee Dee interjected. "Wait a minute. Again? So, who else did he invite?"

"Well, just me."

Dee Dee released a sneaky chuckle. "He has a crush on you, don't he?"

"Stop it. He has no interest in me outside of work. So, can we drop it."

Dee Dee raised an eyebrow in disbelief. "Really?"

"Yes, really. That is the farthest thing from his mind. All he talks about are budgets and profits. But if Daniel would only treat me half as well as Mr. Stanley did, that would be enough."

Dee Dee asked, "Speaking of Daniel, how did he take the news about the trip to Atlanta?"

"All I can say is not good. Not good at all. He was upset about it but I told him, I was still going."

Liz cheered that I took a firm stance with him. "Good for you! It's about time you stood up to that big bully."

Little did they know that in that moment, I only felt the venom of fear as it paralyzed my thoughts and emotions. I knew he was still upset. So upset that he didn't even go to church with me yesterday. I went by his house to check on him but he was not home either.

"So, he's not talking to you again? Right?" Dee Dee lifted an eyebrow, creating wrinkles in her forehead.

"It's worse than that."

"Worse?"

Liz drew a quick breath. "Worse?"

"Yeah, worse. He was so mad that he almost hit me when I told him."

Liz's mouth opened wide as silence held her thoughts captive.

"What!" Dee Dee's conversation went further. "If he lays a finger on you, I will come down there and jack him up and I mean that!"

Liz replied, "And you know she is crazy enough to do it."

Dee Dee started punching the air with her right fist. "You've got that right. Just call me, Crazy Dee Dee."

Liz eyes widened. "Tell her, Dee Dee."

"Tell me what?" I asked.

"I know where Daniel was at this weekend."

My head tilted back in relief. "You do?"

"Yeah, I do. You know that Gerald took me out Saturday."

"Yeah."

"And he took me to this fine steakhouse."

"Yeah..."

"Uh, did you know that Daniel was in Dallas, Saturday?"

I rolled my eyes at Dee Dee's words. "He was? Oh, he probably had a business meeting Saturday. So he probably just spent the weekend."

"He wasn't dressed for a business meeting, girl. He had chains around neck and his shirt was almost unbuttoned to his navel. He was with a woman. By the time I saw him, he headed out the front door."

I laughed and flicked my hand dismissively. "You are so suspicious. Even if he was out with another woman, it doesn't mean anything. He could have been out with a colleague or a friend."

As I spoke, I couldn't help but feel a knot in my stomach. I knew that there had been times in the past where Daniel had been less than faithful, and I couldn't shake the feeling that Dee Dee was wrong for spying on Daniel.

Liz interrupted my thoughts. "Hey, Stormie, did you hear what Dee Dee said?"

I shook my head, even though she couldn't see me. "Yeah, I heard her."

Dee Dee piped up again. "Listen, Stormie, I'm not trying to cause trouble. I just think you deserve to know the truth. You're engaged to this guy, after all."

I sighed. "I appreciate you, girl, for looking out for me. But I trust Daniel. And you shouldn't jump to any conclusions."

Dee Dee took a deep breath, unsure of what it would take to convince me. "I told you she wouldn't believe it."

"You are not going to talk me out of marrying the man of my dreams so forget it. Hey, I'm pulling into the parking garage so I'll talk later, okay."

As a pulled in a parking spot, I began to think about the message that I had heard the Pastor preach yesterday on "The Trouble with Gossip."

I only had only a few weeks before my vacation and I had a lot of work to do. *Where is that file?* I shuffled through the stacks of files on my desk. I knew that I had to finish auditing several files before the annual audit in August. The same month I was getting married. *What was I thinking to plan a wedding in the same month?*

I attempted to call Daniel once again, but my frustration grew as he continued to ignore my calls over the weekend.

"I've been trying to reach you since Saturday night. Why haven't you been answering?" I asked when he finally picked up the phone.

"Do you really expect me to be eager to talk to you right now? You need to get your act together after what we discussed on Friday night," he replied, his tone laced with annoyance.

I bit my lip. "I understand that you're upset," my voice shaking with part cautiousness and part concern. "But ignoring me isn't going to solve anything. We need to talk about this."

"I don't think there's anything left to talk about," Daniel replied coldly. "You made it clear that you're more interested in going on vacation with your friends than in building a future with me. Not only are you stupid but you are selfish."

"That's not true." I protested. "I just need some time to relax before the wedding. That all I want."

Daniel snapped. "I don't have time for games, Stormie Brown. I need a woman that is concerned about me and my career. If you're not willing to support me in that, then maybe you are not the right woman for me or any other man."

His words stung deep down.

My voice raised barely above a whisper. "I love you. Even when we are married, I will always prove that to you. I will see you when I get back from vacation."

"I tell you one thing, once we are married, I will show you who is the boss and you will see what it's like when you don't do what I tell you to do." With that, he hung up, leaving me wondering what he meant.

CHAPTER TEN

Stormie

My vacation couldn't come soon enough. Before I zipped up my suitcase, I took a final inventory. *Shorts, two blouses, bathing suit, flip flops, tennis shoes, sandals, two dresses, socks, underwear, bras, make-up bag, toothbrush, toothpaste, vitamin packs. I hoped I didn't forget anything,* I thought.

I zipped it up and grabbed my purse and the plane ticket from the dresser. I felt bad about not saying goodbye to Daniel but quickly set my sights on Atlanta.

With my bags checked at the outside counter, I made my way inside the airport, ready to embark on our adventure.

Dee Dee and Liz's decided to drive to Houston but first stopping in College Station to visit relatives for a few days. We made plans to meet at the airport so we could fly out from Houston.

Dee Dee looked straight at me as she spread her arms wide towards me for a hug. "Girl, are you ready for some sun, fun, and men!"

"Dee Dee, don't start. You know I am not looking for a man on this trip or any other trip. Please don't forget, I'm engaged."

Dee Dee laughed as she switched her hips toward the security gate, "I won't forget it as long as you don't." Dee Dee was quite a character and the queen of flirtation. She had mastered it. It came natural to her. But she just did it for fun and was never serious. However, she looked for opportunities and took it when a man would let her. If a man actually took her up on her offer, I know she would run away like a scared rabbit. She knew that she already had a good man.

She was always on the lookout for a good time, while I preferred to keep things low-key. As we made our way through security, Dee Dee couldn't resist flirting with the male TSA officer. I cringed at her shamelessness, hoping that she wouldn't get us in trouble. Despite our different approaches to vacationing, we always enjoyed each other.

Dee Dee looked at the male TSA officer, winked, as she held both arms straight up in the air. "You can pat me down if you need too."

"No ma'am. Just go through the scanner, please."

I was embarrassed. "Dee Dee, behave."

"Sweetie, are you married?" Dee Dee's question caught the TSA officer off guard as she asked with a mischievous glint in her eye.

Clearing his throat, the TSA officer replied. "Yes, ma'am."

Liz gave her a slight nudge. "Dee Dee, stop playing around before we miss our flight."

Dee Dee stretched out her hand and snapped her fingers at Liz. "I'm just getting warmed up."

As we walked onto the airplane, Liz warmly greeted the captain and the three flight attendants who were some of her co-workers from Dallas area. The flight crew had been flying out of the Houston location that week because of a staffing shortage.

Liz introduced us to them as we looked for our seats in first class.

"Do I have connections or what?"

I look at her in disbelief. "First class? Girl, you have connections."

"Of course. Nothing but the best for my two best friends. They were not booked so my friend at the counter reserved them for us."

When Dee Dee saw our seats, she rushed to the one on the right aisle and plopped down as she fastened the seat belt. When she refused to move over, Liz had to squeeze past her to sit next to the window.

I took the seat across the aisle from them. I eased back against the plush leather seat and relaxed as Liz kept a watchful eye on Dee Dee.

Dee Dee couldn't help but gawk at one of the flight attendants, Marcus, as he made the flight announcements over the intercom. He had a deep, smooth voice that commanded attention and made even the most mundane details sound interesting. Liz nudged her with a smirk, knowing exactly what was going through Dee Dee's mind. Liz had flown with that crew on a regular basis for the past five years.

Dee Dee hunched Liz. "He's cute. Introduce me to him when he comes by."

"Baby, you can scratch him off your list. He is married with eight children and one on the way."

"Eight kids?"

Liz shook her head. "Yes, eight and one on the way," added Liz. I'm going to call Gerald, if you don't behave."

"Gerald knows how I am. He knows I'm a big flirt. He also knows that I don't want anybody but him."

I laughed and informed both of them to wake me up when we get to Atlanta.

Before I knew it, Dee Dee shouted several times. "Stormie, wake up! We are here."

I yawned and caught the end of a conversation of a flight attendant trying to calm a frantic passenger.

Blinking away the remnants of sleep, I glanced around and realized we had reached our destination in Atlanta. Stretching my limbs and rubbing my eyes, I tried to gather my bearings. However, my attention was quickly drawn to the commotion unfolding a few rows ahead. A flight attendant stood by, trying to console a passenger who appeared to be in a state of panic.

The frantic passenger, a middle-aged woman with disheveled hair and a flushed face, was gesturing frantically and speaking in an agitated voice. Her eyes darted around, searching for something with a mix of anxiety and desperation.

I leaned in closer to Liz, who was observing the scene as well. I whispered, my voice filled with intrigue. "What's going on?"

Liz sighed, her tone filled with familiarity. "It's just a case of a misplaced purse. Sometimes passengers are forgetful during flights and they start panicking."

I raised my brow, trying to comprehend the situation. I watched as the flight attendant gently tried to calm the distressed passenger, speaking in soothing tones and offering reassurance. It was clear that the attendant had dealt with similar incidents before and knew how to handle the situation.

Gradually, I began to piece together the puzzle. The woman's initial panic had been triggered by the belief that her purse had been stolen. However, to everyone's relief, it was eventually discovered under her seat, right where she had left it.

Liz turned to me with a knowing smile displayed on her lips. "You see, these cases aren't uncommon," she said, her voice filled with a mix of empathy and understanding. "Flying can be stressful for some people and their emotions can sometimes get the better of them."

I nodded, realizing that the woman's frantic state had been born out of a temporary lapse in judgment rather than an actual theft.

As the flight attendant helped the relieved passenger settle down, the cabin gradually returned to its usual buzz of activity.

I took a deep breath, grateful that the situation had been resolved without any real harm done.

Liz used her credit card points and rented us a hotel suite. It was one of the nicest rooms I had ever stayed in.

"How about we get a bite to eat and go for a swim in the pool when we get back?" requested Liz.

Dee Dee nodded. "That sounds good to me. How about it, Stormie?"

"First let me freshen up."

I went into the bathroom to fresh up and called Daniel to let him know that I had arrived safely but he didn't answer his cell phone. I sent him a quick text: "Just made it to the hotel. Wish you were here. Text me back. Love, Stormie."

As I left the bathroom, Dee Dee was sitting on one of the beds and threw a pillow in my direction. "I bet you were in there texting Daniel."

I gave a guilty chuckle. "I'm sure that he wants to know that I made it." And I was thinking about all the planning I still needed to do for the wedding. I needed to put my house up for sale, Daniel and I needed to open a joint bank account and I still needed to find a wedding dress. It was overwhelming all the things I needed to do with the wedding only five months away.

"So, what is Daniel doing?" Liz chimed in. "Sounds like you are doing all the planning of this thing."

Dee Dee placed her hand on my forearm. "Can we just have a good time without you focusing on him or the wedding?"

"You're right. Why don't we go to that seafood restaurant on the river that you told us about, Liz?"

Liz hoisted herself off the bed, grabbing her purse. "Sounds great. Let's go."

I felt relieved that my friends understood my situation and didn't pressure me to do anything I wasn't comfortable with. As we walked to the rental car, I couldn't help but think about Dee Dee's words. *Was I too focused on the wedding and not enough on enjoying the moment?* Maybe she had a point. After all, this vacation was supposed to be a break from all the wedding planning. I made a mental note to try to relax and enjoy myself, regardless of the wedding preparations that were looming over me. We hopped into the car and drove off to the restaurant. As Dee Dee's favorite song filled the car, the atmosphere shifted and a wave of excitement washed over her.

"Turn the radio up. I love that song," exclaimed Dee Dee.

Liz and I couldn't help but feel a surge of energy as the catchy melody filled the car. With the windows rolled down and the wind tousling our hair, we sang along at the top of our lungs.

As the song ended, Dee Dee turned to me with a mischievous smile. "You know what? This restaurant has a live band playing tonight. We are going to have a good time and not leave until they close the place like we did when we went to California. Remember?"

My eyes lit up, appreciating Dee Dee's contagious enthusiasm. "Yeah, of course I remember."

Liz giggled. "I remember too. They put us out of that place."

As we arrived at the seafood restaurant, the aroma of delicious food greeted us. The smell of fried fish and hushpuppies made my mouth water. The decor was nautical-themed with fishing nets and seashells adorning the walls. We were seated at a cozy booth by the window and the waiter took our drink order. I gazed out at the sunset on the Chattahoochee River while we each perused the menu. The lively ambiance, music, and cheerful chatter added to the anticipation of the evening.

Dee Dee flirted with the waiter, a handsome young man with a charming smile. Liz was scrolling through her phone, checking her social media pages. I was lost in thought, trying to push the stress of wedding planning out of my mind.

Suddenly, my phone rang. It was Daniel. I hesitated before answering, not sure if I was ready to deal with his demands and expectations.

"Hey," I said, trying to sound cheerful.

"Hey, Baby. I just wanted to check in and see how your trip is going," he said.

"It's going well. We just got to the restaurant for dinner."

"Good. Glad you are enjoying yourself. I'm here eating a frozen dinner. But don't worry about me. Just have a good time. Oh, while I have you on the phone, have you made any progress on the wedding planning?"

I sighed. "Not really, I just got in not long ago and we drove straight to the restaurant. So, I haven't had a chance to do much yet."

"Well, I just don't want us to get behind on the schedule."

"I know," I said, feeling the familiar knot of anxiety forming in my stomach.

"Oh, I forgot to tell you that about my job review. My boss couldn't stop talking about what a good manager I was. I love you and see you when you get back."

"Okay, bye, I love you too." I said, hanging up the phone.

Dee Dee and Liz were looking at me with concern.

"Is everything okay?" Dee Dee asked.

"Yeah, it's just Daniel. He's so focused on work and the wedding."

"Girl, like we said, you need to take a break from all that drama from him," Liz said. "Let's enjoy our dinner and then dance our booty off."

I chuckled, grateful for my friends. They always knew how to cheer me up and make me forget about my problems. We ordered our food and continued our conversation, laughing and enjoying each other's company.

Dee Dee flagged down our waiter and flirted shamelessly with him again and he seemed flattered by her advances. Liz and I exchanged amused glances.

As we sipped on our glass of iced tea, I couldn't help but feel a sense of relief being away from Daniel for a little while anyway. I loved him, but our relationship had become so stressful with his constant focus on his career and my role in supporting it.

I turned to Dee Dee and Liz. "Thank you, guys, for inviting me to go on this trip with you. I really needed to get away from everything for a little bit."

Dee Dee grinned. "Of course, girl. That's what friends are for."

Liz nodded in agreement. "And we are going to make sure you have the best vacation ever."

As we enjoyed our meal and conversation, I felt the weight of my wedding planning responsibilities start to lift. Maybe this trip was exactly what I needed to clear my head and find some perspective on my relationship with Daniel.

The next day, we decided to go on a guided tour of the city. Our tour guide, a friendly middle-aged man named Joshua, was full of interesting facts and stories about Atlanta's history. As we drove past the famous landmarks, such as the Martin Luther King Jr. National Historic Site and the Georgia State Capitol, Joshua's commentary brought the city to life.

On the third and fourth day, we wandered through the stores. Dee Dee couldn't resist flirting with every handsome guy she saw. Liz and I decided to take a break and grab some coffee at a coffee bar while Dee Dee continued to shop.

As we sipped our drinks, Liz leaned in and asked, "You seem a little distracted again."

I sighed and looked down at the engagement ring on my finger. "I don't know, I guess I just can't stop thinking about my wedding. It's supposed to be the happiest day of my life, but it feels like there's so much pressure to make it perfect."

Liz reached out and took my hand. "Don't worry about it. You'll have a beautiful wedding, I'm sure of it. But for now, just focus on enjoying your vacation and having fun with us."

I smiled at her and squeezed her hand. "Thanks, Liz. You always know how to make me feel better."

We finished our coffee and rejoined Dee Dee, who was now carrying several large shopping bags.

Dee Dee winked at us. "You guys missed out on some great deals."

We laughed and continued our shopping trip, enjoying each other's company and the sunny Atlanta weather. Even though I was still thinking about my wedding from time to time, I felt a sense of calm and happiness being with my two best friends.

CHAPTER ELEVEN

Britney

Britney had been waiting for this moment for so long and now she was finally alone with Daniel for a whole week. He booked her a flight to Houston and rented a car for her. Her desire for Daniel overpowered her better judgment, as she stepped into the hotel room. Daniel had a towel wrapped around the lower half of his body and beads of water was rolling down his body.

As she sat on the bed, watching Daniel get dressed, she couldn't help but wonder if he had done this before like her. Had he brought other women to this hotel? Was she just another conquest to him? But she pushed those thoughts aside.

"I'm looking forward to dinner," she said, trying to sound nonchalant.

Daniel smiled back at her. "I know you are going to love this place. It's cozy and romantic."

As they left the hotel room, Britney couldn't help but feel a sense of excitement and anticipation. The restaurant was small and cozy, with dim lighting and soft music playing in the background. They were seated at a corner table, and Daniel ordered dinner for the both of them. After their food was served, Daniel leaned in and whispered in her ear.

"I just want to make sure that you know how much you mean to me."

He kept telling her how much he cared about her. He talked about all the things he loved about her, the way she laughed, the way she looked at him, and how much he enjoyed spending time with her.

Britney was swept off her feet by his words and for a moment, she forgot about everything else.

Daniel's phone rang with a ringtone that caught both his and Britney's attention. It was a different ring tone, one she had never heard before. Daniel quickly pulled his arm from around her as he reached for his phone.

"I told you I had a business meeting tonight, baby," Daniel said, his tone slightly apologetic. He listened for a moment, nodding along. "Yeah, I will. Okay. Talk to you later."

As Daniel ended the call, he stretched his arm back around Britney's shoulder, trying to regain the intimacy they had before the interruption.

"Stormie, huh?" Her voice tinged with a hint of jealousy and frustration.

Daniel hesitated, reluctant to delve into the details. "Yeah, it was her," he admitted, not wanting to cause any further tension. "Where were we?"

Britney couldn't help but express her disappointment. "I thought this was our special week together with no interruptions. I can't believe she called, and that you answered her. I thought this was our week together. Just us."

Daniel took a deep breath, trying to find the right words to explain himself. "Hold on a minute, Britney," he said, his tone firm but gentle. "Yes, it is a special week for us. But I also need to answer my phone when it rings. And, well, you must have forgotten that Stormie and I are getting married."

Britney's eyes widened in surprise, and a mixture of emotions washed over her.

Britney shook her head. "Now, I know now that you were never serious about me." Britney couldn't help but feel a mix of disappointment and concern. Her eyes widened in surprise and a mixture of emotions washed over her. She thought that Daniel's would break off his engagement with Stormie by now so the two of them could get married. But she was wrong. She realized that Daniel was still planning on marrying Stormie.

Daniel leaned in closer, his hand reaching out to touch her arm. "But I am serious, Britney. I care about you. You understand that, right? We can keep seeing each other after I am married."

Britney's heart sank as she realized that she had been nothing more than a fling to him.

"I can't believe you would say that. You led me on and made me think that we had something real."

Britney pulled away from his touch, feeling a surge of anger. "You can't have it both ways, Daniel. I hope Stormie knows what kind of man she's marrying."

Stormie

As Dee Dee opened the hotel curtains, sunlight flooded the room, blinding me. I tried to hide under the blanket to block out the brightness.

"Good morning, Buttercup! We're headed to Savannah, Georgia today," Dee Dee exclaimed, her eyes gleaming with excitement.

Liz chuckled. "I haven't heard you call her that since high school," she joked, nudging Dee Dee playfully.

"You two go on without me. I'm going to stay in bed," I groaned. "I'm exhausted from all that dancing last night. I need some rest."

"Not a chance," Liz snatched the covers off me. Dee Dee grabbed one of my legs, and Liz grabbed the other, dragging me out of bed.

"What are you two doing! Are you both crazy?" I protested, feeling disoriented as I stumbled to my feet.

Dee Dee and Liz were determined to take me on an adventure in Savannah. Despite my objections, they managed to pull me along with them as we embarked on a day of exploration and excitement.

As we made our way through the bustling city, I couldn't help but feel grateful for Dee Dee and Liz's enthusiasm. Even though I had been hesitant to leave the comfort of my hotel bed, I soon found myself caught up in the excitement of the day. We explored the historic district of Savannah, marveling at the architecture and learning about the city's rich history. Dee Dee and Liz led the way, pointing out interesting landmarks and sharing anecdotes from their own experiences.

I opened up to them about some of the challenges I had been facing lately and they listened with compassion and understanding. By the end of the day, I felt rejuvenated and energized. I realized that sometimes it takes a little push from the people we love to break out of our comfort zones and experience new things.

Early the next morning, we drove about twenty miles before we arrived at Tybee Island, just as the sun was starting to rise. As we got closer to the beach, the excitement grew. The air was cool and crisp and the water was still calm and peaceful. We could see the ocean in the distance and hear the sound of the waves crashing against the shore. When we arrived, we found a parking spot and quickly made our way to the beach.

As we walked towards the shoreline, we could feel the warm sand beneath our bare feet and the sound of seagulls echoed in the distance. We spread out our beach towels, laid down, and enjoyed the peaceful sounds of the ocean.

Dee Dee and Liz ran towards the water, splashing each other, while I watched from the comfort of my towel. I was content to listen to the sound of the waves.

After a while, I couldn't resist the temptation any longer and joined Dee Dee and Liz in the water.

The salty sea water was refreshing and we laughed as we tried to jump over the waves.

As the day went on, we explored the island, stopping at local shops for snacks and souvenirs. We even visited the Tybee Island Light Station and Museum, where we climbed to the top of the lighthouse and took in the breathtaking views.

After lunch, we decided to head back to the beach to spend the rest of the day. This time, we rented beach chairs and umbrellas, slathered on sunscreen, and set up camp for the afternoon. The waves were perfect for swimming and we laughed and joked as we played in the water.

As the sun began to set, we sat on the beach watching the beautiful colors of the sky change as the day turned into night. Liz took a lot of pictures to remember the trip by and reminisced about all the fun things we did and the memories we made. We sat in silence, taking in the beauty of the moment and the memories we had created.

As we drove back to the hotel in Atlanta, I couldn't help but feel grateful for the amazing memories we had created on this trip. I knew that

I would always remember the time spent with my friends and the adventures we shared together.

As I laid in bed that night, staring up at the ceiling, I reminded myself of the importance of taking time for myself. It had been a reminder that amidst all the chaos and pressure, it's essential to take a step back and enjoy life.

With that, I closed my eyes, taking comfort in the memories of our trip and the knowledge that no matter how busy my life may become, I would always have these moments to look back on and cherish. It was exactly what I needed to clear my mind and enjoy life again. From the late-night conversations to the endless laughter, it had been a truly unforgettable experience.

CHAPTER TWELVE

Stormie

On the plane trip back to Houston, we experienced a lot of turbulence. The unexpected shaking and bouncing of the aircraft sent waves of panic and fear through the passengers. Some screamed, while others held onto their armrests tightly, desperately seeking stability in the chaos. Feeling my own anxiety rise, I closed my eyes, praying and calling upon Jesus for a safe landing. Gripping the edges of my seat, I believed that we would make it through this turbulence unscathed.

Finally, after what felt like an eternity, the plane touched down on the runway and a collective sigh of relief echoed throughout the cabin. The tension in the air dissipated, replaced by a chorus of applause and grateful expressions from the passengers who had endured the harrowing experience together.

As we gathered our belongings, preparing to disembark the plane, Liz took a moment to wave goodbye to her co-workers. With a smile on her face, she exchanged warm waves and shouted, "See you on Wednesday!"

Her co-workers reciprocated the gesture, waving back with a mix of excitement and anticipation of the upcoming flight to Los Angeles with her.

"Can't wait!" one of the flight attendants called out, her voice filled with enthusiasm as well.

With a final wave and a heartfelt farewell, Liz made her way off the plane as we followed her.

As we made our way to the parking garage, Dee Dee eyed me over the top of her car. "Stormie, that turbulence was a sure sign that you shouldn't marry Daniel."

"What are you talking about Dee Dee?"

"God's trying to tell you something," Dee Dee explained. "Buttercup, you just need to read the handwriting on the wall."

Liz giggled and interjected, "Dee, please stop. You're going to make me pee on myself."

Dee laughed. "Okay, okay. But seriously, just think about it."

After a round of hugs and goodbyes, Dee and Liz headed back to Dallas, while I headed home. I refused to believe that it was a sign from God of what was waiting in the days ahead.

CHAPTER THIRTEEN

Stormie

Maybe time apart was what Daniel and I both needed. I enjoyed my vacation but I sure was glad to get home. As I searched for my house key in my purse, memories flooded my mind, taking me back to the day Daniel proposed.

"Stormie Brown, will you marry me? You are the woman I need in my life forever," he said. Tears streamed down my face, and my mascara ran, but I didn't care. I was so happy in that moment. It took several minutes for me to compose myself.

Daniel took my hand. "Are you going to give me an answer?"

"Yes!"

He pulled out an engagement ring from his jacket pocket and placed it on my finger. As he kissed me, it seemed as if we were moving in slow motion. It was so romantic. The way he proposed was like a fairy tale. He was my prince charming, rescuing a damsel in distress from being single.

A shout from across the street startled me when I heard, "Welcome home, Stormie!"

My neighbor, Mrs. Marshall, gave me a quick wave as she picked up her newspaper and headed back inside. Her worn pink robe and oversized pink bunny slippers looked cozy and comfortable. Mrs. Marshall was a sweetheart, always ready with a smile and a kind word. She loved to cook and whenever she made a casserole, she would bake an extra one for me so I wouldn't have to cook for a few days. I opened the door and placed my suitcase on the floor.

After a long flight, all I wanted was a warm shower and a comfortable bed. I needed to unwind before work tomorrow. As I went to grab my phone to check for any missed calls or messages, I saw a text from Daniel.

It read: "Stop by the cleaners tomorrow and pick up my dry cleaning. I have a meeting tomorrow."

I was taken aback. No "welcome home" or "how was your trip?" Just a demand for his dry cleaning. I couldn't believe it. I sighed, feeling disappointed and frustrated. I had hoped for more but knew I couldn't deal with it right now.

As I started to unzip my suitcase, my eyes landed on a large seashell I had picked up from the beach. Memories of the vacation flooded my mind and I smiled.

Reality set in. I had a house to sell and a fiancé who seemed more interested in his dry cleaning than my wellbeing. I shook my head and reminded myself that I needed to focus on one thing at a time. *Tomorrow, I would deal with the dry cleaning but tonight, I'm going to unwind and enjoy being home.*

Upon returning to work on Monday morning, I glanced at the neat stack of five new project folders on my desk. As I was deep in thought, the phone rang, and I picked it up to hear Mr. Stanley's cheerful voice on the other end. He greeted me warmly and suggested we have lunch, calling me his "Favorite employee of the year."

I cleared my throat to steady my voice. "Are you kidding me? I had no idea that I had even been nominated."

Employee of the year had many perks. For one, a closer parking spot, a thousand dollars bonus, and a week off with pay. I couldn't hardly believe that the board of directors had selected me. Seven-five percent was based on performance and twenty-five percent on communication skills.

"No, I'm not kidding. I hope you like Mexican food. See you at eleven thirty outside. Bring the Kenwick and Mitchell files with you."

It was hard, but I managed to wrap up both files and complete a summary report before eleven twenty. I put the folders in my briefcase, grabbed my purse, and made a dash for the elevator.

When I went outside, Mr. Stanley was on the passenger side of a different Porsche. This one was white.

"Guess who's driving today?" he signaled for me to get behind the wheel. I just bought it today."

"Mr. Stanley, I can't drive this expensive car."

"Call me, Justin."

"Mr. Stanley. I mean, Justin, I can't drive your new car."

"Do you have a driver's license?"

"Yes, sir."

"Okay then. Floor it!"

What was his staff thinking as I sped off? I hope this doesn't get around the building. No way did I want to leave the impression that anything was going on between us.

As we took our seats at the restaurant, he picked up the conversation where we left off. Did you have a good time?"

"It was so nice, but nothing as adventurous as your travels around the world. Just a trip to Atlanta."

"I haven't been there in years. Did you go alone?"

"No, I went with a couple of my girlfriends."

"You deserve it."

As I looked into his eyes, there was a spark. I felt something I had never experienced with Daniel. I quickly glanced away, feeling a rush of emotions. As the waiter brought a large bowl of chips and salsa to the table, I reached for a chip, but his hand suddenly covered mine. I froze, unsure of what to do, and slowly pulled my hand back, confident that it must been an accident. My eyes slowly rose from page fifty-eight, looking in his direction.

His only comment was, "It wasn't an accident."

"Sir?" I was afraid to ask him what he meant by that answer.

We continued our conversation over lunch, discussing work, travel, and our mutual love for Mexican food. As we talked, I found myself feeling more and more comfortable with him. There was a sense of ease between us. We chatted like we had known each other forever. We talked about everything from our childhoods to our dreams and aspirations for the future. I was very comfortable around him. I truly enjoyed his company.

Justin decided to drive back to the office so he could demonstrate just how fast his car could go. The engine roared to life and we zoomed down an open road with the wind rushing through our hair. I couldn't help but feel a mix of excitement and nervousness, secretly praying that we wouldn't attract the attention of the police.

To my surprise, the thrill of speed took over and I found myself laughing alongside Justin. The adrenaline pumping through our veins made every moment feel exhilarating as we embraced the freedom of the open road.

As we approached the building, Justin eased his foot off the gas pedal and pulled over to the side of the road. He rummaged through his briefcase and then handed me a comb with a mischievous grin. As he pulled down the visor above my head, I couldn't help but chuckle at his playful gesture.

"Looks like you could use this," with a twinkle of amusement in his eyes.

Curiosity got the better of me and I glanced in the mirror. What I saw made both of us burst into uncontrollable laughter. My hair, tousled and wild from the wind, resembled a bird's nest more than anything else. Stray strands were sticking out in every direction, defying gravity.

As the laughter subsided, I combed through my hair, attempting to tame the chaos. Justin watched. His expression filled with amusement. With my hair now somewhat presentable, we resumed our journey, driving the final two miles towards the building.

When I returned to the office, Janice was waiting for me inside. She spoke in a hushed tone, "Girl, everyone in this building is talking about you."

I raised an eyebrow, pretending ignorance.

"What do you mean?"

"You know what I mean. You driving Mr. Stanley's car."

"How did you find out?"

"You know that word spreads quickly in this place. People saw you driving off with Mr. Stanley and the rumors started flying."

I let out a nervous chuckle, realizing that my attempt to keep it under wraps had failed. "Well, I hope they're enjoying the show," I replied, attempting to brush off the situation with a nonchalant attitude.

"You know people talk around here. So, what's really going on between you two?"

"Like I told you before, Justin and I are just friends and that's it."

Janice looked over her reading glasses. "Justin? So, you are on first name basis now."

As Janice and I continued our conversation, I know rumors and speculations roamed the hallways. While the attention could be overwhelming, I knew deep down that I was capable of handling it with grace and professionalism. After all, I had worked hard to get to where I was and no amount of gossip could overshadow my achievements.

With that mindset, I moved forward, ready to face whatever challenges and rumors came my way. In the midst of it all, I was determined to stay focused on my goals and continue to excel in my career. I needed no favors from Justin to accomplish that.

The phone on Janice's desk rang. "I will be back later so I can get to the truth around here." Janice rushed down the hall and made it back to her desk to answer the ringing phone. "Good afternoon, Miss Brown's office, Janice speaking."

"Hi Janice, this is Michelle."

"I didn't expect to hear from you today."

"I know but I had to call you. Do you remember me telling you that Stormie's fiancé looked familiar?"

"Yeah, I remember."

"Well, about six months ago I saw him in New York."

"So."

"So, he was with a woman but it wasn't Stormie. He was kissing and carrying on with a woman half his age."

Janice's voice rose an octave not totally believing her words. "Are you sure?"

"Positive. I never forget a face. I saw him with my own eyes."

Truth began to settle into Janice's mind. "I need to tell her before she marries him."

"Hold up one minute. Before you do that, let me ask you this. Do you like your job?"

"Yes, I do."

"Do you like your boss, Janice?"

"Of course. She's the best."

Michelle leaned back in her executive office desk chair. "Well, if I was you, I would leave it alone."

Janice surprisingly paused. "You mean not tell her?"

With strong words of caution Michelle added. "I mean, mind your own business. He will just deny it and she will believe him."

"You think she would?"

"I know she would. I have been around long enough and seen everything under the sun to know that it will not end well for you. So just leave it alone."

"Anyway, I was calling to see if you wanted to have dinner tonight at Deb's Grill?"

"Absolutely. I'll meet you there at seven."

Michelle returned her chair to an upright position, "Sounds good. See you tonight."

Even though Janice knew Michelle was telling the truth, she was in a state of disbelief. She could not believe what she had just heard.

CHAPTER FOURTEEN

Stormie

For the past five months, Justin had taken me out to lunch every Wednesday. It had become our little tradition, one that I looked forward to with eager anticipation each week. There was something about Justin that was so different from any man I had ever met before. He was kind, caring, and genuinely interested in everything I had to say. He listened to my concerns, ideas, dreams and he always had something thoughtful to say in return. I felt like I could tell him anything and that he would understand and support me. I found myself feeling more and more drawn to him with each passing week.

As we sat down and ordered our food, Justin leaned forward as he would do every Wednesday and always ask me a question that caught me off guard. "Tell me, where do you like to go shopping?"

I paused, surprised by the question. I had never really thought about it before. "Well," I said, hesitantly. "If it has clothes, shoes, and jewelry, it's on my list."

Justin smiled, approving my answer. "One day, I'm going to take you shopping."

I laughed, not taking him seriously. "You don't have to do that, Justin. I can take care of myself."

"I know you can," he said, as he winked his right eye. "But I want to. It's not every day that I get to take such a beautiful and intelligent woman shopping. Please say you will go."

I blushed at his words and tried to hide it by looking down at my menu. Justin always knew how to make me feel special and I couldn't help but feel grateful for his kindness and attention. As we continued our conversation, I found myself opening up to Justin in a way I had never done with anyone before. He made me feel safe and I knew that he genuinely cared about me.

"Before I say yes, I need to let you know that I'm engaged to be married next month," sounding cheerful as I tried to discourage him from the idea.

"I heard. But you have another option, you know."

As I twisted my engagement ring on my finger, I felt a sense of confusion. The symbol of love and commitment was now making me feel doubt. I didn't know what to believe anymore.

Justin's expression turned concerned. "Stormie, are you okay?"

Taking a deep breath, I shook my head. "I don't know. Me and my fiancé we're having trouble. But at the same time, I made a commitment to him, and I don't want to hurt him."

"Turn around and close your eyes because I bought you something."

I complied with Justin's request and turned around, closing my eyes. I was skeptical about what he wanted to give me, but I went along with it anyway. I was determined to prove him wrong about me having other options besides Daniel. Suddenly, I felt Justin's warm hands on the back of my neck as he fastened something around it. His touch was gentle as he rubbed the length of my neck before pulling his hands away. Chills ran all over me as my whole body clinched. Immediately, I opened my eyes to see a beautiful diamond necklace shimmering in the light. It was simple yet elegant and it took my breath away.

"Justin, it's beautiful," I whispered as my fingers traced the delicate chain.

"Let me see how it looks on you. I hope you like it."

As I turned, I clinched the diamond and looked at him.

"Justin, this is so beautiful," I gasped in amazement. "I cannot accept this."

Justin smiled softly, "Stormie, you deserve to feel loved and appreciated every single day of your life. And I want to be the one to do that for you. You have options, Stormie. You are looking at one right in front of you."

I couldn't help but feel overwhelmed by his words. Tears welled up in my eyes as I looked at him. I nodded slowly, not trusting my voice to speak.

Justin continued, "I feel like I've known you my whole life. I love you, Stormie Brown. I've never felt this way about anyone before."

I took a deep breath and looked at Justin. "I need some time to pray about this and to think things through."

CHAPTER FIFTEEN

Stormie

When I returned to my office, my mind raced with questions. *Could I really break off my engagement with Daniel? How would he react? What would people say? But then again, did I really want to spend the rest of my life with someone like Daniel who didn't treat me with respect and love?*

I spent the rest of the day lost in thought, as mental scales of my mind tipped back and forth, trying to weigh the pros and cons of staying in my current situation with Daniel versus taking a chance on a new path with Justin. As much as the idea of breaking off my engagement scared me, I couldn't ignore the growing sense of excitement and hope that came with the possibility of a happier future. For the first time in a long time, I felt like I had a way out of the mess I had found myself in.

I called Dee and Liz for advice and support and told them what happened during lunch with Justin.

"I knew it! Didn't I tell you, Liz? I told you."

"Yep, she said that your boss was in love with you."

Dee Dee's excitement drew a question. "So, what are you going to do?"

I drew a deep breath. "I don't know right now. I need to pray about it."

Dee Dee seemed puzzled by my response. "Pray about it? What's there to pray about? Didn't you say that the man is gorgeous, successful, rich, and loves you?"

"He is but what about Daniel?"

Liz chimed in. "What about him?"

I took another deep breath and tried to calm myself down before continuing. "I thought I loved

Daniel, but I also have feelings for Justin. What will people think if I called off the wedding?"

Liz spoke up first. Don't worry about what other people think. This is your life, and you deserve to be happy."

Dee Dee chimed in. "Stormie, for the first time in your life you have an opportunity to know real love. There shouldn't be any question in your mind about what to do."

"I know. But there is."

Liz added, "Let me ask you something. What is your heart telling you?"

"My heart is so excited and happy to be around, Justin. He is so kind and so easy to talk to. I think about him all the time. I thought it was just me. I really tried to quinch the feelings I was having for him."

Liz chimed in again. "What is happening is that you are torn between your commitment to Daniel and your own happiness. You know deep down that Daniel doesn't treat you right, but you couldn't bear the thought of breaking off your engagement and disappointing your family and friends."

"You're right," I said, wiping away my tears.

"Stormie," Dee Dee frowned. "Daniel always criticizes and belittles you. He makes you feel like you couldn't do anything right."

"Yeah, but he has never hit me." Sadness covered my eyes. "Doesn't that count for something?"

"Girl, verbal abuse may not be physical but still just as controlling and manipulative. The scars of it are not visible to the naked eye, Stormie. They are hidden deep inside that is slowly damaging your self-worth."

Liz interjected. "Daniel has never treated you right and I couldn't imagine you spending the rest of your life with someone who didn't love and respect you. And Justin, well, he makes you feel alive in a way that you had never felt before."

As the days passed, I found myself constantly thinking about Justin and what our future together could be like. I prayed for guidance and for the courage to follow my heart, even if it meant going against what everyone else expected of me.

As the wedding day approached, Justin had been waiting patiently, hoping for a chance to show me how he truly felt.

Finally, after two weeks, I knew what I had to do. The day of the wedding rehearsal dinner, I made my decision.

The weight of the decision hung heavily on my shoulders. As I dialed Daniel's number, my hand trembled with nervousness. I took a deep breath, knowing that this call would change everything.

My heart rapid fired. "Daniel, we need to talk. It's important."

"Okay, what's going on?"

I knew once I spoke, there was no turning back. "I've been doing a lot of soul-searching and I've realized that I can't go through with the wedding. I can't marry you, Daniel."

"What? Are you crazy, Stormie!"

"I understand how difficult this must be for you to hear."

"You can't just call off the wedding like that, Stormie! We've been together for over five years. I made a lot of sacrifices for you. I thought you were happy."

"No, Daniel, I'm not happy. It wouldn't be fair to either of us to continue down a path that doesn't feel right."

Daniel's face turned to stone. "I don't understand why you're doing this. How can you do this to me? To our future? To my career? I have a promotion even riding on this marriage."

I shook my head, unwilling to change my mind. "It's better for both of us to end things now."

Daniel pleaded, "No, listen. We can go to therapy and work through our issues."

"It's too late for that. "It's over, Daniel. I'm moving my clothes out your house tomorrow and leaving the key under the door mat."

As expected, he began hurling insults. "You're stupid you know that! No one else wants you. You're throwing away your last chance for happiness."

I held my composure. "Goodbye, Daniel. I hope you find the right person for you and your career."

Without saying goodbye, Daniel abruptly hung up the phone.

With a deep sigh, I sat down the phone and leaned back in my chair. His lies, cheating, and verbal abuse I endured was in the past. It was finally over. Despite the sadness and pain of ending a long-term relationship, a weight had been lifted off my shoulders. I felt free, like I could breathe again.

The next day, I went over to Daniel's house to pack up my clothes. I was glad Justin gave me time off work to move back to my house. Janice volunteered to help me, armed with boxes on the back of her truck. We worked in silence, trying to avoid any mention of the canceled wedding or the pain that lingered in the air. As we packed my belongings, memories flooded my mind. Each item held a story, a reminder of the life I had envisioned with Daniel. But now, they were just remnants of a dream that had been shattered.

Janice broke the silence, attempting to distract me from the heaviness of the situation. "This is the biggest Primary Bedroom closet I have ever seen. Look at all the stuff you have in here!"

I managed to smile, grateful for her attempt to lighten the mood. "Yeah, I got the bigger closet in this house but I still needed more space," I replied, my voice filled with a sadness.

Janice pulled up the side of her shirt to reveal a pistol strapped to her waist.

I gasped, shocked by what I was seeing. "Janice, why are you carrying a gun?"

"If Daniel shows up trying to cause trouble, I'm ready for it."

The thought of facing Daniel scared me. "Do you really think he'll come over here?"

Janice patting her gun for emphasis. "I don't know. I wouldn't put anything past him. But I'd rather be safe than sorry."

Janice glanced around the room, taking inventory of all my clothes and personal belongings. "I feel like I'm at a clothing store."

I nodded, a wistful smile playing on my lips. "I know. Can you believe that I gave away half of my clothes and I still have too much stuff?"

After my stuff was boxed up, I began moving Daniel's suits from the Guest Bedroom and hung them in the Primary Bedroom closet. As I transferred the last few suits, my hand brushed against a jacket pocket, and I felt something bulky inside. I pulled out several white envelopes.

To my shock and dismay, the envelope contained credit card and bank statements. As I scanned over the pages, my heart sank further with each revelation. The statements unveiled a web of lies and deceit, showing expenses for trips to exotic locations, hotel stays, and even visits to a hair salon.

Worst of all, there was an unexpected balance of eighteen-thousand dollars in the checking account that Daniel had never mentioned.

Overwhelmed with emotion, I felt a lump form in my throat. Just then, Janice walked in holding a t-shirt that Daniel had bought when we first started dating. Written on it was the words, *I Found My Prince Charming*.

Janice sat down next to me and placed a comforting hand on my shoulder. "Stormie, what's wrong?" she asked softly.

I sat down on the edge of the bed, staring at the papers in my hand. My hand shaking, unable to find the words to express the anger inside me.

I finally managed to say, "Daniel was still cheating on me. Like a fool, I believed him that he had stopped."

As she sat with me, I couldn't help but reflect on the signs of Daniel's infidelity that I had ignored for so long. There were moments when he seemed distant, occasions when I caught him in small lies, but I had always brushed them aside, desperately clinging to the hope that our love would conquer all.

Now, in the midst of the shattered trust, I realized that I had been fooling myself. I had allowed my heart to hold onto a false hope, convincing myself that our relationship could work despite the underlying issues. The truth was that our connection had been flawed from the very beginning and that I had been blind to it.

Before today, I only knew Janice as the efficient and reliable secretary from the office. She was the one responsible for managing my schedule, ensuring all my appointments were in order, and seemingly always in the loop when it came to office gossip. But little did I know, she had a depth of character that went far beyond her professional role. In that moment, Janice became more than just a familiar face in the office. She had shown me her true self—a compassionate, understanding, and caring person.

Janice stayed by my side, patiently supporting me as I sifted through paper after paper, trying to unravel the web of lies that Daniel had spun. With each new discovery, the pain of his betrayal cut deeper. It hurt to acknowledge that Daniel had been so dishonest, but deep down, I felt a twinge of pity for him.

"I can't believe how dishonest he was." My voice filled with a mixture of hurt and anger. "It's painful to realize that he was still cheating on me."

Janice's voice was filled with sincerity. "Stormie, I'm so sorry."

I shook my head. "I can't say that the fact I found out that he betrayed me again didn't hurt. It did, deeply. But more than anything, I feel sorry for him. I'm sorry that he couldn't be honest with himself or with me."

Janice offered a comforting presence. "I fully understand what you're going through. I dated someone like Daniel once. He was a cheater and verbally abusive too. But I learned that sometimes before a person can be rescued, they have to want to be rescued. It took me years of heartache and pain to learn that lesson."

I looked into Janice's compassionate gaze. "You're right. I didn't want to be rescued."

In that moment, I realized that Janice was not just a secretary, she had become a friend and a confidante. It was as if our connection had transcended the boundaries of the professional realm, blossoming into a genuine bond founded on mutual care and understanding.

Her words brought a reminder that despite the pain, I still had Justin, someone who loved me. With Janice's support and the truth now laid bare, I knew it was time to find the strength to move forward and build a life with Justin who really loved and cared about me. After the last box was loaded onto Janice's truck, I took off my engagement ring from my finger and placed on the kitchen cabinet. I locked the front door, slid the key under the door mat, and refused to look at Daniel's house.

As I drove off, Janice followed closely behind in her truck, ready to lend a helping hand. When we arrived at my house, we started unloading boxes.

Mrs. Marshall and her husband, saw us unloading and rushed over to offer their assistance. Their warm smiles and willingness to help lifted my spirits in that difficult moment. Together, we formed a small assembly line, passing boxes from one person to another until they were safely inside the house.

Mrs. Marshall then invited us over for lunch. She had already prepared fried chicken, complete with homemade bread and a fresh salad from her garden. Mr. Marshall kept us entertained with his funny stories. We laughed so much that our cheeks hurt.

After lunch, we helped clear the dishes and thanked the Marshalls again for their hospitality.

CHAPTER SIXTEEN

Stormie

Janice's cell phone call broke the silence as we walked back across the street to my house.

"Hello. Yes, I know who this is. How are you doing? Yes, I would be delighted to go. What time are you picking me up? Okay, I be ready by then. Thank you for calling."

Stormie's curiosity grew as she overheard Janice's conversation.

Janice was grinning ear to ear. "Guess what?"

"What?"

"You know Jeff, Mr. Stanley's personal assistant? He asked me out on a date tonight."

"Really? Are you going?"

"You better believe it. That man is fine! I'm going straight home and get ready. He is picking me up at eight and we are going to see a movie. See you on Monday."

Janice waved goodbye driving off as I unlocked my front door and went inside.

Surrounded by unpacked boxes of clothes and dishes, I plopped down on the couch, grabbed my phone, and began to listen to a podcast message from Pastor Rankin, *Forgiveness: The Key to Moving Forward.* As I allowed Pastor Rankin's message to seep into every corner of my heart and soul, this is what Jesus was trying to convey to every believer. Before, when I said I forgave them, it was just empty words. But now, I really meant them.

Forgive me, Lord. I'm sorry that I have not forgiven my stepfather, Daniel, and myself.

I closed my eyes and confessed out loud. "I forgive you, Victor, for all the pain you brought upon our family. I release the resentment and anger that has burdened me for years."

Next, my thoughts turned to Daniel, the man I loved despite the tumultuous journey we had shared. I acknowledged the hurt he had caused me—the betrayals, the harsh words, and the doubts that had plagued our relationship. But in that moment, I chose to let go of it all.

"I forgive you, Daniel," I whispered, my voice filled with strength. "I forgive you for the times you've disappointed me, for the secrets you kept, and for the pain I had to endure."

I forgave the memories of the trips Daniel had taken with other women, the times he had lashed out with hurtful words, and the moments he had doubted my love.

"I release the resentment and grant you and Victor my forgiveness."

Each word of forgiveness became a stepping stone on the path to my own healing. I realized that forgiveness wasn't about condoning the actions of others or forgetting the pain they had caused. It was about releasing the grip of resentment and sailing in waters of healing and growth.

With each word, a weight was lifted off of my shoulders, and I felt a renewed sense of freedom. As I embraced the power of forgiveness, I knew that the journey wouldn't end here. It was a continuous process.

As I spoke those words, I felt a profound shift within my being. The weight of their past transgressions against me began to dissipate, replaced by a sense of peace, restoration, and confidence in myself. Forgiveness, I realized, was not just an act of mercy towards others, but also a gift from God that was offered so that I could be free too.

My phone rang, interrupting my thoughts. Justin, invited me to join him for an unforgettable evening at the theater. He had managed to secure tickets to the highly sought-after play, "Love's Unyielding Flame," in the vibrant theater district of downtown Houston. I really wanted to go because of all the good reviews I had read about it.

Dee Dee and Liz, had seen it a few months ago during its run in Dallas and couldn't stop talking about it for weeks. Liz promised me that the play would definitely transport me into a realm of raw emotions, to immerse me in the struggles and triumphs of this courageous couple. Now, I had the opportunity to see it firsthand.

I rummaged through my desk drawer to find the review I have saved from a magazine. John Weatherspoon, Critic for the Houston Arts Society and Theater Review wrote, "It is a love story about a young couple whose love was put to the test when the girl's father vehemently opposed their blossoming relationship. The father, blinded by his own prejudices, deemed the young man unworthy of his daughter's affections. However, their love only grew stronger in the face of adversity, fueled by an unyielding determination to be together."

As I continued reading, I was drawn even more into the story.

"Their path was strewn with thorns, beset by countless obstacles that sought to tear them apart. Faced with the father's relentless opposition, he made a selfish decision, uprooting his family and relocating from America to Italy, naively hoping to sever the unbreakable bond shared by the young couple. But distance proved futile in extinguishing the flame of their love."

I turned the page as the Play Critic wrote, "Undeterred by the vast expanse that separated them, the young man refused to succumb to despair. With unwavering resolve, he embarked on a relentless pursuit to find his beloved, vowing to defy time and space itself. It was a testament to the enduring power of love, a declaration that no obstacle could quell the fire burning within their souls."

Weatherspoon ended his review by writing, "The writing brilliant and a true masterpiece."

As I got ready, I couldn't help but feel a bit nervous like a high school girl on her first date.

I chose a simple yet elegant dress and put on my favorite pair of heels. As I looked at myself in the mirror, I took a deep breath and reminded myself that I deserved happiness and love. When Justin's limousine arrived, his chauffeur opened the door, I slid in next to Justin. He looked handsome in his suit and my heart fluttered when I saw him.

I smiled at him. "I want to make sure I say and do the right things tonight."

His word comforted me as he held my hand. "You don't have to impress anyone tonight, not even me. Just be yourself."

When we arrived, we were escorted to his private box. During intermission, Justin and I talked about our hopes and dreams for the future. He shared his passion for business and how he wanted to use his success to help others. I opened up to him about my desire to start a non-profit organization that would provide hope to abused women.

Justin looked deeply into my eyes. "Stormie, I want to spend the rest of my life with you. Will you marry me?"

Without hesitation in my voice. "Yes."

He slipped a beautiful diamond ring onto my finger. It was a moment that I would never forget. And I turned the page to the beginning of a new chapter in my life.

Love, I realized, couldn't solely be measured by the absence of anger. It was a multifaceted tapestry woven with trust, respect, and understanding. From that moment on, my love for Justin continued to bloom into something beautiful. I was finally with the man who loved and respected me the way I deserved.

Janice found out that Daniel had been transferred to another state shortly after we broke up. He never got his BIG promotion. Rumor has it that he staged a fake online wedding ceremony to impress his family, inflate his ego, and to be showered with expensive gifts.

Stormie

Six months later, Justin and I stood at the altar, exchanged wedding vows and promised to love each other forever. Dee Dee and Liz both were my maids of honor and it was such a joy to have them by my side on my special day.

It was such a beautiful event, filled with family, friends, and co-workers who were overjoyed to see us tie the knot. We danced the night away, basking in the glow of our love and the promise of a wonderful future together.

A year has passed since our wedding. I marveled at how Justin's entrepreneurial spirit had thrived. He dedicated himself to expanding his companies, leveraging his skills and resources to create new opportunities and ventures. However, amidst his achievements, he also recognized the importance of giving back to the community.

He formed a non-profit organization *The Healing Hearts with Love Foundation* and appointed me Director so I could share my passion to make a difference in the lives of women who had endured the pain of abuse. My organization was dedicated to providing support, resources, and a safe haven for victims. It was a role that held immense responsibility but also filled me with a sense of purpose.

He moved me and my staff of fifteen into the empty offices across the hall from him. The empty offices were quickly transformed into a bustling hub of compassion and healing as my dedicated staff and I worked tirelessly to create a nurturing environment for those in need. Of course, Janice was still my secretary.

My heart swelled with joy as I contemplated the exciting future ahead, not only for Justin and I, but also for our good friends Dee Dee and Liz. The revelation that Dee Dee's boyfriend had a twin named Darrell added an intriguing twist to our journey. Especially when the twins proposed to Dee Dee and Liz at the same time. Little did we know that this unexpected connection would pave the way for a truly unique celebration. Plans for a double wedding began to take shape, igniting our imaginations and fueling our anticipation. They took up Justin's offer to hold the ceremony at our ranch in Austin, Texas and he would pay for all the expenses as a wedding gift.

As I looked back on my journey, I could only thank God for all that He had done for me and in me. Justin was the pillar of strength, respect, and honor that helped me overcome my past.

As Justin and I stood on the balcony of our beautiful home in The Woodlands, Texas, we held hands. In that moment, I realized that sometimes the greatest love stories are the ones that come from unexpected places. The ones that start with a simple lunch, words of encouragement, or just having someone with a listening ear. I knew that I was blessed enough to have found that kind of love, a love that had rescued me in so many ways and had given me a life beyond anything I thought possible. I couldn't help but feel grateful to God who had led us to this moment. I had come a long way from that first business lunch invitation with Justin and the fear and uncertainty that had once filled my heart. He had been there for me, guiding me, supporting me, and loving me unconditionally. As the sun began to set on the horizon, casting a warm glow over everything in its path, Justin leaned in for a kiss.

Together, we would continue to sail together in waters filled with love and hope that unfolded with every journey.

www.ingramcontent.com/pod-product-compliance
Lightning Source LLC
Chambersburg PA
CBHW060745180626
46818CB00002B/449